Yaakov and the Treasures of Timna Valley

NATHANIEL WYCKOFF

Book 2 in the Peretz Family Adventures Series

Text copyright © 2015 by Nathaniel Wyckoff

Cover art by Jeanine Henning
www.jeaninehenning.com

ISBN-13: 978-1518717796
ISBN-10: 1518717799

DEDICATION

This book is dedicated to my beloved children, who inspire me daily, and to my ever-faithful wife, Janna, my truest friend.

I also dedicate this book to my wonderful, loving parents, who grounded me with a true sense of identity and a love of Judaism, and who sparked within me the love of storytelling that made this entire effort possible.

CONTENTS

ACKNOWLEDGMENTS

My beloved children continue to inspire my storytelling ventures. Whether I'm inventing a story on the fly, telling them Midrashic tales about the weekly Torah portion, or reading to them about the latest adventures of Tintin and others, sharing stories remains one of our most special experiences together.

My parents laid the very foundation for my writing and for everything else that I have ever accomplished. From a very young age, I heard fascinating stories from both of them, rich tales drawn from our vast Jewish heritage and creative, invented stories that entertained and educated my two dear brothers and me. My mother has always had a talent for making Judaism come alive, and scarcely a bedtime passed without a fantastic tale from my father. I am forever indebted to them for sparking my lifelong interest in my Jewish identity and tradition, and in storytelling in general.

Friends too numerous to name have supported my writing ventures, asked me when the next book is coming out already, and encouraged me to continue. Thanks to all of you for believing in me.

Of course, I must thank our Creator, for implanting within me the ability to concoct tall tales and the urge to write them down for others.

Reviews of *Yaakov the Pirate Hunter*

"★ ★ ★ ★ ★ Nathaniel is a creative writer with a vivid imagination. Not only does he create vivid worlds you're excited to explore, but he does it in a way that children can grasp and understand the magnitude of the novel concepts and story lines he weaves."

"★ ★ ★ ★ ★ I read Yaakov the Pirate Hunter with my kids and it was a remarkable experience. Each night my kids waited for me at bedtime to find out what new and exciting storylines would be revealed on that night."

"★ ★ ★ ★ ★ I love the mix of the old and the new. Ordinary people, like us, are living in a modern, futuristic world. Mr. Wyckoff blends the two very well. The story, itself, moves along at a cracking pace and will be easy to read for any middle grade reader. It is a marvellous story that all children will find entertaining and enjoyable."

"★ ★ ★ ★ ★ The story is very well-written. Kids will enjoy reading this book themselves [instead] of having it read to them- especially those who love hi-tech adventure!"

"★ ★ ★ ★ ★ I loved this book! It contains such high adventure, suspense and humor. I look forward to the next book!"

Join my email list, for updates on future books:
www.peretzadventures.com

1 THE BULLY'S UP TO SOMETHING

"Get that fishing hook out of my face!" exclaimed Yosef Peretz, looking up for a moment from the spherical toy in his hands. "You can hurt somebody with that thing!"

Yosef held a clear plastic ball, about the size of a basketball, in his hands. Inside the ball was a track that formed a maze. The goal was to maneuver a tiny silver ball through the maze by turning the sphere in various directions.

He shoved away his older brother's fishing rod and went back to the maze. It was another slow Friday afternoon in the scorching L.A. summer, and Yosef didn't seem to want to do much but recline on his bed, playing a game while a fan in the corner blew air onto his face.

"Sorry," answered Yosef's older brother, Yaakov, "I was just looking for my tackle box."

"Well, it's not in here," replied Yosef, in an annoyed tone. "And why do you even need it now?

We're not going fishing until Sunday."

"Whatever," answered Yaakov. "I probably left it in the garage."

He ran from Yosef's room and headed to the backyard. His younger sister, Rachel, was there, riding her bicycle in laps around the concrete driveway in front of the garage. She was the youngest of the three Peretz children. Rachel was constantly full of life, and ready to join in her brothers' activities. She always seemed to look up to them.

On seeing her brother, she quickly brought her bike to a stop. "Hey, Yaakov!" she called. "Look how fast I can go!" Then, she began pedaling again, as furiously as her seven-year-old legs would allow.

"Wow," Yaakov responded with a smile, on his way to the garage, "you are getting fast. You might even beat me some day."

Rachel stopped her bike again. "I bet I can beat you today. Let's have a race right now!"

"I can't do it right now, Rachel," answered Yaakov, grasping the garage door handle and beginning to pull it upward. "I have to find my tackle box."

Rachel got off of her bike and followed her brother into the garage. "But that's boring! Let's do something fun."

Upon entering the garage, Yaakov stopped and turned to his sister. "I'll tell you what, Rachel. You can help me look for my tackle box, and once we find it, I'll go for a ride around the neighborhood with you."

"Okay," she answered, with a trusting smile.

Yaakov began walking around the cluttered room, in search of his little plastic box of fishing supplies. *Why does this room always get so dusty?* he wondered briefly.

After a few minutes, Rachel lifted a small, rectangular black box with a plastic handle. "Found it!" she declared triumphantly "It was on the floor, right here, next to Buzzing Bill! Hey, let's not have a race. I changed my mind. Let's just play with Buzzing Bill instead. We haven't turned it on in a long time."

Buzzing Bill was one of the Peretz family's five robots. It was constructed as an android-like figure, with a touchable display screen on its mid-section and a small satellite dish on its goofy-looking, reddish head. All five of the Peretz family's robots now stood silently in a row, against one wall. The Peretzes had actually owned six robots at one time, but Yaakov tried not to spend a lot of time thinking about the sixth. Built for two-way electromagnetic communication, Buzzing Bill had caused the Peretzes a lot of satisfaction and a lot of trouble several weeks earlier.

Yaakov gave Rachel a sympathetic look. "Rachel, I know it's fun to mess around with our robots, but Imma doesn't let. She said she wants me to stay away from them the rest of the summer, and I don't want to get in trouble. So, let's find something else to do."

As often done in Jewish families, the Peretz children called their parents "Imma" and "Abba," the Hebrew words meaning "Mother" and "Father."

"Oh, come on," Rachel pleaded. "Let's just turn it on for five minutes and keep looking for those signals. Remember when you said Bobby the Brute probably sent a message with his little black box? Maybe we can read it!"

Remember? thought Yaakov. *How could I possibly forget?*

A completely unplanned adventure had begun just a month earlier in the Peretz family's yard. After their climbing robot's fall from the roof, the kids and their father discovered a pirates' treasure map stored in its head. Dilip Sitoop, their robot dealer, had fearfully placed it there when trying to hide from a gang of pirates whom he had just helped to burglarize a wealthy man's home in Santa Barbara. The map eventually led the Peretzes to a spot in the desert, where the kids, their father, and their digging robot unearthed a box full of precious stones and other valuables. After this discovery, Yaakov outwitted the pirates and helped the others return it to its owner, billionaire Aharon Sapir.

A short while later, Mr. Sapir sent the Peretz family to the tiny Tunisian island of Djerba, just off the coast of Africa. There, Bobby the Brute, a member of the pirate gang, was out to steal an ancient Torah scroll from the island's Jewish community. The pirate was planning to sell that religious item to a mysterious character named Rahulla Allijabulla.

Right before their trip to Djerba, Yaakov used Buzzing Bill to track the pirate's ocean voyage from Santa Barbara to Djerba. Then, the whole Peretz family literally hunted down Bobby the Brute. They staked him out at Djerba's historic synagogue one Saturday night, caught him in the act, and alerted the local police.

To foil the pirate's plan, Yaakov had to give up Digital Drudge, a robotic personal assistant that he had built all by himself. He used Digital Drudge to block Bobby the Brute's secret tunnel into the synagogue, and Bobby the Brute ended up smashing the robot to pieces while trying to get past it. By wasting a few precious minutes destroying a robot, Bobby the Brute gave the police plenty of time to arrive at the scene of his crime.

Just a few moments before being arrested, Bobby the Brute managed to mess around with a little black box that he owned, possibly sending someone a message.

Since the night of Bobby the Brute's arrest, Yaakov had felt very anxious to check Buzzing Bill. He had accidentally left the robot turned on throughout their two-week trip to Djerba. If Bobby the Brute actually had used his black box to send a message, then just maybe, while pointed at Djerba, Buzzing Bill had picked up something.

As usual, it was hard for Yaakov to say "no" to his younger sister. "Look. After we got back from Djerba, Imma told me that she didn't want me to mess with pirates anymore, and she doesn't let us play with Buzzing Bill. I guess we can take a really quick look at what was going on that day from Djerba, right here in the garage, and then turn off the robot and do something else. But no more after that, all right?"

Rachel's face lit up. "All right!"

Reluctantly, Yaakov turned on Buzzing Bill and watched it come to life. "Hey there," came its robotic voice, "what's the buzz?" *Couldn't they have made it sound a little more normal*, wondered Yaakov, *like the automatic voices built into our cars?*

Whispering, Yaakov instructed Buzzing Bill to search its databanks for any public radio transmissions that had been sent from the area around Djerba on the night of Bobby the Brute's arrest: Saturday, July 5, 2025. Yaakov told the robot just to show him transcripts, printed words stating what others had said aloud, instead of actually playing the broadcasts; his mother could walk outside at any minute, and if she heard any spoken voices from Buzzing Bill, then he and Rachel would be in trouble. The two of them huddled over the robot's display screen and scrolled through sports scores, weather reports, ads for strange foods and clothing, and boring news about local events. Much of it meant nothing to them, because it was in Arabic, a language that none of the Peretz children understood. After about two minutes, Yaakov noticed a couple of strange titles printed in English: "DJERBA ENGLISH RADIO SPREADING OUT" and "HAPPY WEATHER TIMES."

"Happy weather times?" asked Rachel, with an impish grin.

"Shhhh!" whispered Yaakov. "You want Imma to find out?"

"Sorry," she whispered back. "Can we read that?"

"Okay," answered Yaakov. He slowly scrolled through a paragraph or two of broken English, describing the cloudless skies of Djerba in July and other pointless information. The two children occasionally chuckled at the incorrect English sentences that they read. Eventually, something caught Yaakov's eye.

"Look at this! It's weird," he stated sharply, in as close to a whisper as possible. He pointed to the screen and showed his sister a short passage that appeared to be a poem:

A high of 27,
No real chance of rain,
A week of sunny mornings and days,
Cloudless skies will stay till Tuesday,
And warm breezes every night,

Put on sunscreen from UV rays,
And also for the kids too.

"What kind of weather report is that?" wondered Yaakov aloud, while Rachel laughed to herself, with a hand covering her mouth. He stared at the poem for a few moments. Soon, a curious pattern seemed to leap off the screen. "Anacapa!" he exclaimed.

"What?" asked Rachel.

"Look, Rachel! If you put together the first letters of all of the lines of that poem, you get a word. It's the word 'Anacapa!'"

"What does that mean?" she asked.

"It's the name of an island," explained Yaakov. "Remember those pirates from Santa Barbara? Abba told me they were living in a cave on Anacapa Island. What if Bobby the Brute somehow sent the name of the island to someone?"

"Why would he do that?" asked Rachel.

"I don't know," answered Yaakov.

Just then, he heard the sliding glass door of the house open. Quickly, he reached behind Buzzing Bill and flipped its power switch. Its monitor and lights instantly went dim. Yaakov and Rachel turned around and saw their mother, Leah Peretz, walking outside. She wore a bright blue hat adorned with pink and yellow flowers, and held a little paper in her right hand and some rolled-up dollar bills.

"Hello, kids!" she greeted them.

"Hi, Imma," the two children each greeted their mother.

"What are you kids doing in the garage?" she asked.

"Well," answered Yaakov, "I couldn't find my

7

tackle box anywhere in the house, so I came outside and started looking for it in here."

"And I found it!" announced Rachel.

"Oh, good," said Leah, "you're planning ahead for our fishing trip on Sunday. Let me know if you want to do anything else that day, too. For now, I need you run to the market for me and pick up a few things. Here's a list, and that should be enough." She held out her hand toward Yaakov.

Yaakov walked out of the garage and approached his mother.

"Sorry I'm being so primitive," she said, as her son took the paper and cash. "It's just a piece of plain old paper, not an app or something."

"That's okay, Imma," answered Yaakov. "I'll just hitch the horse and buggy, and we'll be on our way."

"Very funny, Yaakov," retorted Leah. "Maybe someday I'll catch up to you and jump into the twenty-first century."

"Can I come, too?" asked Rachel.

"Sure," answered her mother. "The two of you can ride your bikes there. And bring your backpack, Yaakov. We're out of plastic bags, and some of the stores aren't even selling them anymore."

The two children pedaled their bicycles down the sidewalk of a residential street, on their way to a local store, Dan's Kosher Market. Yaakov rode a greenish bike built for typical boys of his age and size. On his shoulders, he wore his black backpack, now containing his tackle box and various trinkets. To his right, Rachel kept up with her brother, riding her much smaller pink bike with its attached bell and basket. About three blocks from their home, they began to approach a wide, shady tree that grew near an intersection and cast long shadows across the sidewalk and an adjacent lawn. That tree was a familiar neighborhood landmark. Whenever he saw it, Yaakov knew to turn right in order to reach the local stores in which his family liked to shop.

Suddenly, a strange-looking boy jumped onto the sidewalk from behind the tree, landing right in front of Yaakov and Rachel and blocking their path. Yaakov and Rachel abruptly stopped their bikes.

"Going somewhere, buddy?" asked the boy, placing his hands on Yaakov's handlebars. His voice sounded slightly deep, yet still childish.

Yaakov recognized the bully, and felt an immediate surge of irritation on seeing him this afternoon. Nobody seemed to know this boy's real name. He was simply known by a bizarre nickname: Plavarto. Apparently, the boy had chosen that label for himself, hoping that it sounded scarier and more threatening than his true name. Plavarto was about half a year older than Yaakov, several inches wider, and a lot sloppier. Today, his light brown hair was a mess, as usual. Dark brown stains of chocolate and reddish remnants of ketchup or salsa streaked his face. He wore a dirty, faded T-shirt advertising a ten-year-old ride at a local amusement park, along with badly ripped and faded blue jeans. His mean, yet dopey, facial expression screamed, "Give me a break. I'm trying to look tough, all right?"

Plavarto was not a very successful bully. His usual tactic was to stop other children in their tracks, demand chocolate or other goodies from them, and threaten that they'd be sorry if they crossed him. Though many younger children found Plavarto physically imposing, he was not exactly a model of fitness. Also, Yaakov didn't exactly find Plavarto to be the sharpest knife in the drawer. He usually seemed to be at least one step behind his potential victims, and it wasn't very difficult to outsmart him. Occasionally, Plavarto managed to dream up some cockamamie scheme to cheat a poor victim out of some money, toy or treat, but those plans usually went sour. It was rumored that Plavarto had once spent time in a juvenile detention facility over a botched incident at a shopping mall involving a Hershey bar and another child's frozen yogurt.

Despite Plavarto's clumsiness, Yaakov wished he didn't have to put up with him today. "Yeah, we're going to the market," he answered Plavarto, defiantly. "Now get out of our way."

"Get out of our way," mimicked Plavarto. "Now, why would I want to do a thing like that?"

"Because I said so, Plavarto. Let go of my bike!"

"Because you said so?" asked Plavarto, in a mocking tone. "Like I care. I wonder what Skinnyso thinks." Then, he turned and faced the tree for a moment, still gripping the handlebars of Yaakov's bike. "Hey, Skinnyso! Come here!"

With a low growl, Plavarto's black adult Rottweiler emerged from behind the tree and walked straight over to the two Peretz children. Yaakov had seen this dog now and then, trailing its owner as he trudged around the neighborhood. Skinnyso crouched in front of Rachel's bicycle and stared at her. Rachel quietly stared back.

Skinnyso? wondered Yaakov. *Who names a pet "Skinnyso?" Did someone once call Plavarto a "fatso?" What a thin-skinned bully!* Before Yaakov could say another word, Plavarto continued his harassment.

"This guy says I should let go of his bike," said Plavarto. Then he raised his voice, and seemed to give his dog a code. "What do you say, Skinnyso?"

Skinnyso began barking loudly and repeatedly at Rachel.

"Stop that!" she yelled.

"Quiet your dog and let go of my bike!" shouted Yaakov. He wasn't about to have his day ruined by a bully, and wasn't going to let his sister be intimidated by this dope and his bothersome pet.

"Let go of your bike?" asked Plavarto, while his dog continued to bark. "Oh, okay, I'll just take something else. What's in the bag?"

Keeping his right hand on the handlebars, Plavarto grabbed hold of Yaakov's backpack with his left hand and started trying to pull it off of Yaakov's right shoulder. Of course, Yaakov pulled it back. Plavarto tried again, pulling harder. After struggling with Yaakov for another moment, Plavarto grabbed the backpack's zipper, opened it a few centimeters, and stuck his fist inside. Yaakov then yanked the backpack away from Plavarto with all his might. At that moment, he remembered something about Plavarto's dog.

"I said leave us alone!" exclaimed Yaakov.

With a quick motion, he then loudly rang the bell attached to Rachel's bicycle. Skinnyso instantly stopped barking. Yaakov rang the bell several more times, and the dog began to whimper. After a few more rings, Skinnyso got up and started to run away, in the direction of the Peretz home.

"Hey, what are you doing to my dog?" hollered Plavarto. He seemed to forget about Yaakov and

Rachel, let go of Yaakov's bike, and began to chase after Skinnyso as speedily as his unfit legs could carry his overgrown body.

"How did you do that?" asked Rachel.

"It was simple," answered Yaakov, closing his backpack. "Skinnyso's afraid of doorbells. A few times, I've seen Plavarto and Skinnyso hanging around in front of other people's front doors right when guests show up and ring their doorbells. Skinnyso always gets scared and starts running away. So, I figured that bike bells must scare him, too."

The children rode on to the market, where they bought the foods on their mother's brief list. All of those items ended up in Yaakov's backpack. As they passed the familiar shady tree on their way home, Yaakov heard Plavarto's voice from behind it.

"I did what you said! Now, where's my chocolate?" Plavarto thundered.

Yaakov stopped his bike about fifteen feet in front of the tree, and then Rachel stopped hers. Yaakov looked at his sister and put his finger to his lips. "Shhhh," he whispered.

Both children slowly turned to take a look at the tree. Plavarto sat on the grass behind it, holding a walkie-talkie. Skinnyso sat by his side.

The walkie-talkie made a hissing noise, which was soon interrupted by a grumpy, unfamiliar male voice. "I told you a thousand times already, fool! Meet Freddy on Sunday morning at the airshow. Don't forget to be in the right spot."

Plavarto pushed a button and asked, "How do I know you're really gonna be there?"

"Look," answered the voice, "it's very simple. I'll

spell it out for you one more time. You show up at the Van Nuys Airshow at 10:00 on Sunday morning. You're gonna pick up the light brown box from the big green trashcan in front of the Drone Demo. You'll carry the box to the Drone Hangar, and meet Freddy there. He'll be wearing blue overalls and a yellow T-shirt. Give him the box, and he'll give you your chocolate. Got it?"

"Of course not," answered Plavarto, with a bewildered look on his face. "How am I supposed to have the box if I didn't go to the airport yet?"

"I meant, did you understand me, you nitwit?" responded the voice, in an irritated tone.

"Yeah," said Plavarto. "He'd better be there, and he'd better have all the chocolate. Or else!"

"Or else what?" asked the voice.

"Just or else," said Plavarto. "And I'm Plavarto, so he'd better not mess this up."

"Don't you mess up," snapped the voice. "See you on Sunday."

"Wait, who's gonna meet me there, you or Freddy?" asked Plavarto, sounding confused again.

"Meet Freddy at the Drone Hangar a few minutes after 10:00 with the brown package. Good bye." More hissing then came from the walkie-talkie, and Plavarto turned it off.

As they pedaled home, Rachel and Yaakov discussed what they had just seen and heard.

"What do you think Plavarto's up to?" Rachel asked her brother.

"I don't know," answered Yaakov, "but I don't like the sound of it." *What a weird boy he is*, thought Yaakov.

13

The whole incident sounded very strange and very unusual for Plavarto. What, indeed, did Plavarto have in mind? Why was he in touch with some strange adult? Why were they communicating by walkie-talkie? And what were they plotting to do at the Van Nuys airport? A scheme involving a suspicious package in a garbage can at the airport didn't sound very innocent. Whatever Plavarto was planning, he had to be stopped!

Yaakov needed a scheme of his own. He didn't think it was any use to confront Plavarto. Plavarto wasn't likely to spill the beans; he would probably just deny the whole conversation with some huffy, sarcastic remarks. Most likely, Plavarto didn't even know what was in the package, and didn't care. Plavarto never really seemed to care about anything. Yaakov had to uncover Plavarto's plan, and he knew that he couldn't do it alone.

When they reached their front yard and the concrete walkway that led to their front door, Yaakov remembered one of his parents' oft-repeated safety tips: "If you see something, say something."

Yaakov stopped his bike, got off of it, and ran through the doorway. "Imma!" he called.

"Hello, Yaakov," she answered, coming out of the kitchen to greet him. "Did you get everything on the list?"

"Yeah," he answered, slightly short of breath, while removing his backpack from his shoulders. "And I have a great idea for Sunday morning!"

2 A SHOWDOWN IN VAN NUYS

Their white, self-driving SUV pulled itself into a parking space at Van Nuys Airport's FlyAway Bus Terminal. From there, it was a brief walk into the airport. Leah and Yehuda Peretz had planned a pleasant family Sunday with the kids. They would enjoy the Van Nuys Airshow in the morning, and then drive over to nearby Bielenson Park for fishing in Lake Balboa and play. As soon as the Peretzes had parked, a young, unshaven man with reddish, shoulder-length hair approached their vehicle, carrying a stack of white envelopes. He wore a light blue, collared T-shirt bearing the words "Van Nuys Rockin' AirFest '25 – Back in Blue" and a nametag that read "Lou." Lou casually stuck an envelope under the vehicle's right windshield wiper, and then walked on to the car in the next spot. Yaakov thought something looked funny about Lou, but soon dismissed that thought and stepped outside the SUV. There was no need for his backpack full of fishing gear, so Yaakov left it in the vehicle.

Following the signs and the crowds, the Peretzes found the ticket booth, bought some tickets and then made their way to an outdoor viewing area, where rows of folding chairs had been set up for the spectators who now began to gather for the 10:30 Drone Demo. As the flyers announced, the Drone Demo was expected to be a spectacular flyover of the latest drone aircraft, officially known as "unmanned aerial vehicles," or "UAVs." UAVs, also known as drones, are airplanes that fly without pilots. They were first invented for military use; for example, the U.S. Air Force may send a drone to a distant location to drop bombs on specific targets. Drones can also be used for purposes that are not military, such as delivering packages. Though some drones are large enough to hold heavy bombs, others may be as small as toy airplanes.

Drones had been banned from air shows for many years. The Federal Aviation Administration, or FAA, refused to allow them, due to the foolish and dangerous antics that the owners of drone aircraft often liked to pull. For example, such offenders used to fly their planes over forest fires to photograph them, thereby getting in the way of the firefighters who struggled to put out those fires. Finally, after many crackdowns that took place over the decade leading up to today's airshow, the FAA began warming up to the idea that most drone aircraft owners were sane, responsible people, and that it was safe to allow them to participate. The Van Nuys Airport celebrated that decision by reserving a special hangar for a number of UAVs that were scheduled to take off from a runway and then perform some impressive stunts.

On this overcast Sunday morning, Yehuda Peretz led

his family to the front row of seats. Yaakov sat on a folding chair, with his parents on his right side and his siblings on his left. He checked his watch. It was a few minutes to 10:00, and there was no sign of Plavarto. Yaakov looked around, and began to wonder whether the neighborhood bully really planned to show up.

Soon, people of all ages were occupying the rows of seats behind the Peretzes. The spectators were a typical, peaceful crowd. Adults chatted with each other about how this was the first airshow in the San Fernando Valley in nearly twenty years. Children nagged their parents for snacks, and complained about how boring it was to wait so long. A few of them whined that waiting for the show to start was even duller than walking around and looking at the airplanes that sat parked nearby. Some in the crowd, young and old alike, chattered on their phones, while others played with toys, read books, or just waited.

After about five minutes, Yaakov's doubts about Plavarto vanished. Yaakov happened to look to his left just in time to notice the bully's arrival. He walked slowly through the crowd, along with his parents, whom Yaakov had never seen before. They both seemed to be worn-out hippies, sporting the same disheveled look that was Plavarto's usual style. Plavarto and his parents found some seats a few rows behind the Peretz family. Yaakov quickly turned his head and faced forward, not wanting to be noticed. Then, he waited ten seconds and secretly glanced backward to spy on Plavarto. He repeated that action after another ten seconds.

"Why do you keep looking back there?" Yehuda asked his son.

"Plavarto's here," Yaakov answered.

"So what?"

"He might actually try to do what he was planning."

"Just sit and relax," said Yehuda. "The show's going to start soon."

Yaakov couldn't relax. He looked back again, and saw Plavarto getting up from his seat, holding a banana peel. While Yaakov watched, Plavarto walked about thirty feet away from the seating area. He approached a pair of large, colored recycling bins, a blue one for artificial trash and a green one for food garbage. Plavarto stood near the green bin and looked around, as if to make sure that nobody saw what he was doing. Then, he looked into it and reached inside it with both hands. He pulled out a package about the size of a bakery cake box, wrapped in tan-colored paper. Yaakov couldn't believe it. Plavarto really was up to something! The bully stood up straight, held the package close to his body, and looked around again. Yaakov's eyes met those of Plavarto.

"Hey you!" shouted Plavarto, in a grumpy, annoyed tone. "Get away!" Then, he turned around and began to run.

Yaakov stood up and faced his parents. "I'll be right back."

"What?" asked Leah. "Where are you going?"

"Chasing Plavarto. I can't let him get away."

"Yaakov," said Yehuda, calmly, "forget about Plavarto. They're about to start the show."

"No," answered Yaakov, impatiently. "I have to go and see what he's doing. Let me just quickly go and see what he's up to, and I'll come right back."

"Here," said Leah, "take my phone." She handed

Yaakov her smartphone.

"Thanks, Imma," said Yaakov, taking the phone and placing it in his pocket.

"You're welcome. And don't get too close to that boy. He's bad news."

Yaakov easily spotted Plavarto. His run was about as fast as Yaakov's slow jog, so it was easy for Yaakov to track him. Yaakov followed Plavarto at a careful distance, so that Plavarto wouldn't realize he was being chased.

Plavarto led Yaakov all the way to the drone hangar. It was a long building with plain, whitish walls, a high roof and a wide entranceway. Today, the building was open to the public, and a modest crowd of interested visitors streamed in and out of it. The drones were to be on display until 10:20. A couple of uniformed officers of the Los Angeles Police Department, or LAPD, patrolled the area on bicycles, while a security guard at the hangar's entrance kept watch on all who entered and left. When he was close to the hangar, Plavarto slowed down from a jog to a walk. He casually entered the building, carrying the tan package under his arm. Yaakov reached the entrance about half a minute after Plavarto. He paused, counted to ten, and then followed the other boy inside.

The hangar was stocked with a long line of unmanned aircraft, parked in preparation for the upcoming show. Some of the planes were being checked by mechanics or touched up by cleaning crews. From the outside, each drone simply looked like a small, typical airplane without windows. Yaakov tried to blend into the crowd, walking from plane to plane and pretending to examine each one, as he secretly continued following Plavarto and watching his every move.

Finally, Plavarto brought his package to the last drone in the row. As Plavarto reached that plane, Yaakov managed to hide behind a cement column supporting the building. That last drone was a grayish jet with "Goleta Gadgets Express" painted across its side in bright red letters. A swarthy man stood next to the plane, leaning against it and holding a socket wrench. At his feet lay a black toolbox. The man fit the description given by the stranger on the walkie-talkie on Friday afternoon: blue overalls over a yellow T-shirt. On his greasy outerwear, the man wore a nametag that read "Fred." His hands were covered by a pair of gloves. To Yaakov, something looked eerily familiar about this guy. Had he seen him before?

Plavarto approached the greasy man, who greeted him with a simple nod. "Here, Fred," said Plavarto, handing Fred the package.

Fred took the box without a word. He turned around, walked over to the airplane, and squatted down next to it. Then, he began pulling tools out of his toolbox and hurriedly tinkering with the body of the airplane. He didn't manage to work for long, though, before Plavarto stepped close to him and began to disrupt him.

"Hey Fred," he demanded, "where's my chocolate?"

Fred looked up at Plavarto momentarily. "What chocolate?" he asked, obviously annoyed.

On hearing Fred's voice, Yaakov froze. The man in the greasy overalls was Powder-keg Fred, one of the six pirates whom he and his family had encountered in Santa Barbara earlier that summer! What was he doing out of jail?

"I was supposed to get some chocolate for doing that!" yelled Plavarto, ignoring Fred's "shush" gesture. "Raul promised! He said I was gonna get four big boxes full of Hershey bars and two big chocolate rabbit bunnies. Now you better give it to me, or..."

"Or what?" asked Fred. "You'll say, 'You better give it to me' again?"

Yaakov quickly turned and ran, while the two of them continued arguing. He had to alert the police, and quickly. At least one of the six pirates who had robbed the Sapir estate earlier that summer was now out of jail, possibly up to no good at Van Nuys Airport, and Plavarto was helping him! *What's in that tan box, anyway?* Yaakov wondered, as he ran outside.

He soon found and approached a uniformed LAPD officer who rode a bicycle across the asphalt at a fairly slow pace. On his standard black uniform, the officer wore a name badge with the name "WILSON."

"Excuse me, officer," said Yaakov, as calmly as possible.

"Yes?" replied the officer, stopping his bike.

"There's something going on in the drone hangar," replied Yaakov. "I saw a kid pull a suspicious package out of a trash can and bring it in there, to a mechanic. He's tinkering with one of the planes. And I'm pretty sure I saw that guy getting arrested a few weeks ago."

"Show me," said Wilson.

Feeling triumphant, Yaakov led Officer Wilson into the drone hangar, walking at a brisk pace while the officer rode his bike. Wilson followed Yaakov to the Goleta Gadgets Express aircraft, where Plavarto and Powder-keg Fred were still bickering over Plavarto's rightful chocolate. Plavarto now stood by the jet with his foot planted firmly on Fred's toolbox. The mysterious package lay on the floor, several feet away from him. A crowd of about a dozen people had now assembled in front of the pair, watching their drama unfold. Several of them were children, who grinned and snickered while listening to the argument drag on.

"I'm warning you, kid!" said Fred. "This is your last chance. Step away from the jet or I'll carry you away myself. Now move."

"*Now move*," mocked Plavarto, without budging.

Officer Wilson stopped his bike. "Hey, you, in the overalls! What's going on here?"

"This guy's not giving me my chocolate!" shouted Plavarto.

Fred faced Officer Wilson. "Nothing, officer. We're just having a little…misunderstanding."

"Well," replied Wilson, "Let's see if we can figure this out. You guys are holding up the show. What's in that box?"

"Oh, you mean that brown one?" asked Fred, pointing to the tan package

"Yes," answered Wilson, "the brown box over there."

Fred shrugged. "Just some stuff for the plane, that's all."

"Let me see your ID," ordered Wilson.

Yaakov stepped away from the ruckus and approached the cement column that he had found earlier. Leaning against it, he used his mother's phone to call his father. "Abba," he said, after they had exchanged greetings, "I'm in the drone hangar. Plavarto's here, too, getting into a fight with a weird guy. I think he's one of those pirates we saw in Santa

Barbara."

"What?" asked Yehuda, sounding shocked. "Are you serious, Yaakov?"

In the background, Yaakov heard his mother's voice ask, "What's going on?"

"Yeah," Yaakov answered his father, "I'm serious. I already found a cop and told him, and now he's talking to both of them. You'd better tell Plavarto's parents, 'cause this looks really bad. They might want to know about something like this."

"Okay," answered Yehuda, "we'll be right over. Just stay where you are, and don't get involved."

Several minutes later, Yaakov's family arrived. Yosef and Rachel excitedly began to question Yaakov about all that he had just witnessed. They were followed soon by Plavarto's parents, who ignored the Peretz family altogether and pushed their way to the front of the crowd now assembled around their son and Powder-keg Fred. Meanwhile, several members of the LAPD bomb squad appeared on the scene to deal with the suspicious package. While trying to answer his siblings' questions, Yaakov continued to observe Plavarto's predicament from afar.

"Pistachio Almond!" called Plavarto's mother, her gravelly voice filled with dismay. On hearing her voice, Plavarto became visibly stiff and looked in his mother's direction with a grimace. Then, he looked away from her, defiantly.

Officer Wilson finished interrogating Powder-keg Fred, and turned to face Plavarto's parents. "Folks, is this your son?"

"Yes, officer," answered Plavarto's mother. "Pistachio Almond, don't worry. We're right here! Just talk to the nice man in the black uniform and everything will be fine."

"Yeah," added his father, in a singsong voice, "it'll all be okay."

Yaakov couldn't help himself. "Pistachio Almond?" he wondered aloud. *Poor guy*, he thought. *If my name were Pistachio Almond, I'd change it to something like "Plavarto," too.*

Plavarto shot an angry look directly at Yaakov. "Shut up, you little weasel!" he hollered.

"Pistachio Almond?" Yaakov repeated, in wonder.

"You're just a little nothing! And you better not spread that around," threatened Plavarto, "or I'll…"

"You'll what?" challenged Yaakov.

Plavarto silently made a fist with his right hand, raised it, and waved it at Yaakov.

Yaakov shrugged. "Whatever you say, Plavarto."

Officer Wilson asked Yaakov and his family to remain in the drone hangar, so that he could discuss the morning's events with Yaakov after questioning Plavarto and Fred. Next, he called for two additional officers to help him manage the situation. He then told the crowd of onlookers that there was nothing to see there, and that they should please enjoy the rest of the airshow. As the crowd quickly left the scene, Yaakov listened carefully to the answers given by Powder-keg Fred and Plavarto. Soon, he was able to piece together a story that explained Plavarto's strange behavior.

Plavarto had no interest in pirates, planes or plots. His main goal these days was to obtain as much junk food – preferably chocolate – as possible, for as little effort as possible. So, when a strange man named Raul approached Plavarto in the park one day and asked him to do a little favor in exchange for a huge amount of chocolate, Plavarto couldn't resist. It was simple, really. All he had to do was to pick up a package from a trashcan at the airport and deliver it to a guy named Fred. Then, he would be rewarded. Raul had insisted on communicating with Plavarto only by walkie-talkie. Plavarto never asked why, and didn't care. It never occurred to him to ask Raul for his last name, either. Having carried out his end of the deal, Plavarto now expected to be paid in chocolate, and refused to budge until receiving his due reward.

Fred's side of the story was more worrisome. After a mysteriously early release from prison for "good behavior," Powder-keg Fred had badly needed to find a job. Raul had contacted him and offered to hire him as an all-around handyman and mechanic; he would be sent out to do odd tasks here and there, as Raul needed. None of those jobs required Fred to dress up as a pirate, and that was fine with him. Today, he was to receive a package from a kid, open it, and place its contents into a special compartment on the outside of a jet at the Van Nuys Air Show. Raul had arranged for Fred to have a phony ID card, so that he could pretend to be from a jet repair company. Fred claimed that he didn't actually know what was inside the package that he had received from Plavarto. The bomb squad managed to get it open, and discovered that it contained nothing but a parachute. Fred insisted that he had no idea why Raul needed a parachute to be inserted on a pilotless airplane; the whole time, he had simply followed orders without questioning them.

Finally, Officer Wilson left the two of them in the care of his fellow officers and spoke privately to the

Peretzes about what they had seen and heard. Yaakov recounted all that had happened the previous afternoon, from the time that Plavarto had bullied him and Rachel on the sidewalk to the moment that he had seen Plavarto pulling a strange package out of a garbage can and carrying it away. He was sure to tell about all that he could remember of Plavarto's strange walkie-talkie conversation.

When Yaakov was finished, Officer Wilson commended him. "Good work, son," he said, with a smile. "You spoke up at just the right time." Then, he turned to Yehuda and Leah Peretz and exchanged contact information with them.

A tall man with broad shoulders and an Air Force-styled outfit suddenly appeared on the scene. "Hey," he announced, "I heard about the holdup. What's going on over here, and when can we get this show on the road...I mean, in the air?" He chuckled to himself for a split second, and then introduced himself as Roger Divins, Captain of the Van Nuys Drone Squadron.

Officer Wilson greeted the newcomer and briefly explained the situation.

"Well," said Captain Divins, grinning from ear to ear, "it sounds like this quick-thinking young man managed to break up a fight and save the Drone Demo at the same time. It's time to reward you for a job well done, and I have just the right thing in mind. Follow me, family."

The Peretzes followed Captain Divins to an office attached to the back of the drone hangar. It was a small, barely decorated room, containing some desks, chairs and several control consoles with display screens. Captain Divins opened a desk drawer and pulled out a life-sized, bright orange parrot.

"Ooh, a pet bird!" exclaimed Rachel. "Can we really have it, Imma? We can keep it in a cage in my room. But we can share it, too."

"Imma," said Yosef, flatly, "I don't want a pet bird."

Captain Divins chuckled again for a moment. "Folks, this here bird is no ordinary pet. I know it looks a lot like a parrot, but it's not even a real bird. It's a new invention: the Spy Squawker. Now, take a close look at its eyes."

He held the Spy Squawker in front of the children's faces, and pointed to the round objects located in the spots where a live parrot's eyes would be.

"Those are camera lenses!" said Yosef, loudly. "How do you use them?"

"It's really simple," explained Captain Divins, patiently. He pulled a black box out of the drawer, and placed it into Yosef's hands. The box included a small joystick, a display screen and several buttons. "You use the remote control to fly the parrot through the air. The cameras film whatever you point them at, and the bird sends continuous video signals to the controller. You just watch the pictures on that screen. You can even record them, save them on a thumb drive, whatever."

"Wow! Thank you," said Yosef. Then he turned to his parents. "Can it be for all of us, not just Yaakov?" he asked.

"Sure," answered Leah. "It can be a family toy. You kids will have to share it."

The three children looked at each other and exchanged yeses.

"This is a lot cooler than our slow-moving robots at home," said Yosef to Yaakov.

"That thing's probably not very fast," countered Yaakov, in a matter-of-fact voice. "Anyway, it doesn't do as much as our robots."

"Kids, no fighting," warned Yehuda. "Now let's thank Captain Divins and go enjoy the rest of the show."

The rest of the airshow was enjoyable, indeed. Despite the brief delay, the Drone Demo was eventually launched. The Peretzes sat on folding chairs and watched as many spectacular vehicles flew over the crowd. Some of them were military surveillance planes, like the Northrop Grumman MQ-4C Triton and the Boeing Phantom Eye. Others included passenger aircraft able to take off, fly to destinations and land without pilots or co-pilots. There were also some tiny public safety planes built with sophisticated sensors. Such drones were used by police forces to locate criminals, or to inspect oil pipelines buried under the permanently frozen soil (known as "permafrost") in the Arctic. Of course, the Goleta Gadgets Express eventually took off, flew around, did some flips in the air, and landed with no trouble at all.

The Drone Demo was followed by some breathtaking stunts performed by live pilots. A woman named Allie Swensen flew a small, bright red jet vertically to a stunning height and then descended quickly, twisting her plane in several corkscrew motions as she did.

As Ms. Swensen pulled off some additional daring feats, the show's announcer explained that pilot's approach to handling fear. "Allie has often been asked whether it's scary to pull off those amazing upward climbs. Her classic answer was one that she gave to an interview two years ago at the Wings Over Camarillo airshow. She said, 'I push the future out of my mind and forget about how I got where I am. Then, I'm free to concentrate fully on what I have to do right now. Every moment is another "now" to be lived to the fullest.'"

Yaakov thought about that quote as he and his siblings strolled around the airfield to admire several additional planes that sat on the ground. *If I only focus on what's happening right now, I never have to be afraid of anything.* He turned over that thought in his mind while heading back to the family SUV with his parents and siblings.

The kids climbed into the vehicle, Yaakov holding onto the Spy Squawker while Yosef carried its controller. After buckling his seatbelt, Yaakov picked up his backpack from the floor and placed it on his lap. Yehuda started the car's engine and muttered, "Bielenson Park" into the tiny microphone built into the steering wheel.

Moments after the car pulled itself out of its parking space, Yehuda's phone rang. The words "Call from UNKNOWN" appeared on the small display screen attached to the dashboard. Yehuda answered the phone. "Hello?"

"Going somewhere?" replied a deep, sinister-sounding voice over the car's speaker system, for all to hear. It sounded familiar to Yaakov. Where had he heard that voice before?

"What?" asked Yehuda. "Who is this?"

"You can just call me...Raul," replied the voice. "I hear you're on your way to fish this morning. Lake Balboa is so nice this time of year. But I wouldn't eat any of that fish. You know what? I have a different destination in mind. So, instead of stopping at the park, why don't we just take Balboa Boulevard all the way to the freeway?"

"No," replied Yehuda, in a stern tone, "we'll be stopping at the park. Now who in the world are you, and how do you know our plans? Is this another crank call from one of the kids' wacky friends?"

"You'll go where I want you to go," snapped the stranger. "I've taken control of your vehicle, so don't even bother switching to manual mode. Don't expect your doors and windows to behave, either."

"What?" asked Yehuda, sounding astonished. He began to flick the switches of the vehicle's doors and windows, furiously.

"Now, just relax," continued the stranger. "Think of yourselves as my guests. I invite you to come and join me today for a little get-together on Anacapa Island. We'll have a chat about that business in Djerba a few weeks back."

"What are you talking about?" asked Leah, in a demanding tone. "Who are you and what do you want?" She then looked at Yehuda. "Yehuda, just hang up and call 9-1-1."

"I wouldn't do that if I were you," replied the strange voice. "It wouldn't be very safe for Tzadok Sapir."

"Tzadok Sapir?" demanded Leah. "Why? What have you done to him?"

Tzadok Sapir, the grandfather of the billionaire Aharon Sapir, was a scholarly gentleman living in the Sapir family's Santa Barbara estate. Originally from Djerba, he had moved to California to build his wine business. Raul, whoever he was, must be connected somehow to the pirates who had burglarized the Sapir mansion in Santa Barbara several weeks earlier.

The vehicle reached the intersection of Sherman Way and Balboa Boulevard, then turned left. As the mysterious stranger on the phone had predicted, the vehicle soon passed Bielenson Park and Lake Balboa completely.

"Let's just keep this conversation pleasant," replied the stranger. "Here's all I ask you to do, and nobody gets hurt. You're on your way to Ventura Harbor. Now, under your windshield wiper you'll find an envelope with five tickets for a half-day cruise to Anacapa Island with Sailing Saway's Island Voyages. My associate, Louie, placed them there for your convenience. Your boat leaves at 2:30. All I ask is that you get on board and sail to Anacapa, then meet me at a cozy little sea cave. There are two tour guides on the boat, Captain Saway and Leroy Caramel. Leroy will be leading the main tour of the island. Just follow Captain Saway, instead, for a little detour to our meeting place. I want to ask you folks a few questions about what else Djerba might have in store for an enterprising…collector. Be on time, if you ever want to see Tzadok Sapir again."

3 TRAPPED!

After their mysterious captor hung up, the Peretz family sat in silent shock for several moments, as their once-reliable vehicle continued its smooth, automatic journey. They soon merged onto the 101 Freeway. To Yaakov, the SUV now felt like a prison. His parents both began making repeated attempts to use their phones to dial 9-1-1. Each time, they were greeted with an annoying recorded message about all circuits being busy. Then, they decided to start calling relatives and friends in order to ask them for help; each of those calls also failed, with the phones simply playing useless messages about busy circuits, rather than making ringing sounds or allowing actual communication to happen. It was obvious to Yaakov that the circuits were not really busy, and that other people had no trouble at all making calls; Raul was to blame for the phony error messages. Of course, all of the Peretzes continued trying to open the vehicle's power windows and locks, only to be disappointed each time. They were now trapped in their own car, being driven to a destination that they did not want to visit, with no way to stop or to ask anybody for help.

At least we won't be thirsty, thought Yaakov, reaching into the ice-filled cooler by his feet and taking out one of the homemade fruity smoothies that they had packed that morning. His was mango-flavored.

"Abba, where are we going?" asked Rachel. "Why did we pass the park?"

"We're taking a different trip today," he replied, facing her, smiling and sounding calm. Yaakov couldn't believe his father's ability to remain cool under these circumstances.

"Where?" she asked. "To fish somewhere else?"

"You'll find out in a little while, Rachel dear. It's a bit of a surprise."

Questions began to flood Yaakov's mind. Why had Raul (if that was, indeed, his real name) mention fishing when he had first called? Even if he could control the car's computer from far away, and could read its destination, how did he know about the family's plan to fish in Lake Balboa? There were plenty of things to do at that enormous park, and most people didn't go there to fish. Also, if all Raul wanted was to ask the family some questions about Djerba, then why didn't he just ask them while they were on the phone? Did this supposed trip to Anacapa Island have something to do with the strange message that Yaakov had read that morning on Buzzing Bill's screen? How did Raul even know about the family's earlier trip to Djerba? And what in the world did Tzadok Sapir have to do with it?

At least one thing was immediately clear to him: this

mysterious Raul had some way to eavesdrop on the family's private conversations. He must have bugged one of them or their car, sticking a listening device into a hidden spot, so that he could hear whatever was being discussed. *How could he have bugged us?* Yaakov wondered. *We have no idea who this guy is, and he's probably never met any of us. And who in the world is he, anyway?*

Yaakov closed his eyes and began to recall all that had happened recently, connect the imaginary dots that led from Friday to Sunday. He and his sister had biked to the market on Friday afternoon, and had briefly been interrupted by Plavarto while on the way there. They had shopped without running into any problems, and then overheard Plavarto's walkie-talkie conversation on the way home. That voice! The creep who had talked to Plavarto on Friday afternoon sounded just like the man who had called Yehuda's phone. Also, Plavarto had admitted to the police that a stranger named Raul had offered him chocolate as a reward for his cooperation. And on Friday, Plavarto had managed to stick his fist into Yaakov's backpack...

Quietly, Yaakov unzipped his backpack and began to rummage through it. He slowly began to empty it, removing each item and silently placing it onto his lap, near the Spy Squawker. At the very bottom of the pack, his fingers felt a strange little metallic object. He slowly pulled it out and examined it. It was a thin, shiny silver-colored disc, about as wide as a quarter and as thick as a nickel. On its face were a couple of little buttons, with some tiny switches and dials. The words "On/Off" and "Volume" were imprinted next to those items, in even tinier black letters. This object was an electronic listening device, commonly called a "bug." Plavarto was the only person outside the family who would have had the chance to place a little object like this one into Yaakov's backpack. He had to be the culprit.

Yaakov quickly opened one of his backpack's outer pockets and pulled out a pen and a small piece of paper. He scrawled the words "We've been bugged." Then, he held up his note and tapped both of his parents on their shoulders. When they turned to look at him, he showed them the note and held his right index finger in front of his closed lips. His mother's mouth opened, and her eyes widened in surprise. Next, with a mischievous facial expression, Yaakov began to wave around the bug in his left hand and the note in his right hand. His siblings stared at him.

"Are you serious?" asked Yosef, on seeing the note.

Yaakov nodded.

Before Yaakov could do anything else, Yosef quietly grabbed the bug from his hand, held it near his mouth, and spoke the words, "I wonder where we are going to today," in a slow and loud voice.

Rachel then reached toward Yosef, with her hands open. He dropped the bug onto her right palm. Fighting a giggle, she brought the bug close to her mouth. With her other hand, she pulled a noise stick out of her little handbag. The noise stick was a plastic tube with one open end and one closed end, containing a small object.

"I don't know," Rachel pretended to answer her brother. "Let's ask our pet guinea pig." She held the noise stick right in front of the bug and flipped it. The stick made an obnoxious groaning sound. Then, she flipped it the other way, producing another loud groan. After a few more groans, Yaakov held out his hand and motioned with his fingers for Rachel to hand him the bug. Right after receiving it from his sister, Yaakov held the bug in front of his mouth and blew a loud raspberry into it, prompting both of his siblings to start laughing. Then, it was his turn to speak into the bug.

"We're coming for you, Raul," he said, trying to make his voice sound as deep and threatening as possible.

Grinning mischievously again, Yaakov dropped the bug onto the vehicle's floor and stepped on it. He stepped on it again, harder this time, trying to crush it. He heard a satisfying crunching sound. Next, he picked up the bug and tossed it to Yosef. Yosef caught the damaged device and dropped it on the floor next to his own feet. Then, he stepped on it, too. While Rachel chuckled, Yosef picked up the wrecked gadget and threw it to her. She caught it, dropped it into her strawberry smoothie and began to shake the drink hard. After about twenty seconds, she stuck three fingers into the thick, pinkish liquid and pulled out the mangled contraption. She then snapped it into two pieces and triumphantly held up both halves for all to see.

With the secret listening device now discovered and destroyed, Yaakov felt free to say whatever was on his mind. "I think I know what's going on with that Raul character, whoever he is," he began.

"All right, Yaakov," answered Leah. "Tell us." She and the others looked expectantly at Yaakov while he explained things as he understood them.

"Raul must have something to do with those pirates from Santa Barbara, the ones that broke into the Sapirs' mansion. Remember when I said that the guy arguing with Plavarto at the airport looked just like Powder-keg

Fred the pirate?"

"Yes," replied Leah.

"Well," continued Yaakov, "I don't think he's the only pirate who made it to Van Nuys. The guy who put the envelope on our windshield looked a lot like a pirate who called himself Red Louie. He had red hair, just like that pirate, and his nametag said 'Lou.' Besides that, I just think I recognized him."

"Yeah," offered Rachel, "I thought that man looked like one of those mean pirates."

"Maybe the character who called us isn't even really named Raul," suggested Yehuda. "Maybe his real name is Rahulla, as in 'Rahulla Allijabulla' and he's out for revenge. I mean, we blew his $50 million crime a few weeks back, so now he's looking for a way to recover his loss by looting some other valuable property. Besides, how would he know about our trip to Djerba unless he was there? We haven't told a lot of people about it."

Rahulla Allijabulla was the Tunisian collector who had apparently hired Bobby the Brute and his fellow pirates to steal the Djerba Jewish community's ancient Torah scroll. By foiling the pirates' plot, Yaakov and his family had both stopped the theft from occurring and deprived Mr. Allijabulla of the next prize in his collection. They had also saved him $50 million that he had wanted to spend on the stolen artifact, but he probably had expected to sell it on the black market for even more than that amount.

That rhyming name, thought Yaakov, *is kind of weird. It's probably made up; 'Rahulla Allijabulla' just sounds a little too silly.*

"Yehuda, are you saying that Rahulla just used

Plavarto to get to us?" asked Leah.

"It's definitely possible," answered Yehuda.

"But what does he want from us?" Leah wondered aloud.

"And why do we have to ruin our day with this silly detour to Anacapa Island?" grumbled Yosef. "He could just ask us whatever he wants and leave us alone. What's over there, anyway?"

At his brother's mention of Anacapa Island, Yaakov cringed. He wondered whether it was a good time to say something about the silly poem that he and Rachel had read on Friday afternoon. True, a weird message that just happened to spell out "ANACAPA" with the first letter of each line might be an important clue. On the other hand, saying anything about it might get him in trouble with his parents. He decided to compromise. He would tell his parents what he suspected, without causing himself any problems.

"I know what's over there," replied Yaakov. "Pirate headquarters. Remember what we learned about those pirates: they were living in a cave on Anacapa Island before they were caught. You know what? I think Raul, or Rahulla, is planning to do something really bad with those pirates."

"You're right, Yaakov," snapped Leah. She sounded serious, almost angry. "It's a trap, and we're not falling into it. That's it. We're done with pirates. As soon as this car is parked, we're getting out and finding a way home. I don't care if I have to smash those windows. We'll get new phones, or find a pay phone – if there are any left anymore – and we'll tell the authorities about Sabba Tzadok." She referred to the elderly man by the affectionate label used by his grandson, Aharon Sapir.

"Sabba" is the Hebrew word meaning "grandfather."

Yaakov's mother had a point. There was no sense in walking straight into someone else's trap. Yet, Sabba Tzadok might be in real danger; if they didn't show up at all, Raul might actually follow through with his threat. There had to be a way to foil Raul's trap without getting caught in it.

"Imma," said Yaakov, "I have an idea. Can I tell you it?"

"Sure, Yaakov."

"We can take that trip to the island," said Yaakov, "and even go that meeting spot." Then, he held up the Spy Squawker with both hands. "Our way."

"What do you mean?" Leah asked her son, squinting and sounding suspicious.

"We'll get on the boat and sail to the island, but we'll never actually meet with Raul. Once we get there, we can pick a hiding place and then launch the Spy Squawker. We'll fly it around, taking pictures all over the place, until we find Raul and see what he's up to. Then, we can call the cops to tell them what he's done."

"Yaakov," said Yosef, "we've never actually seen this guy. We have no idea what he looks like, so how would we know when we've seen him?"

"How many people can there be hiding in caves on Anacapa?" countered Yaakov. "The bird will just fly all over the place until we see someone hiding in a cave, and then we'll call the police. Maybe he's even got Sabba Tzadok tied up in a corner, with-"

"All right, Yaakov," Yehuda interrupted, "we get the point. But we don't even know where Sabba Tzadok is. We need to alert the police as soon as we can. So, here's what we'll do. As soon as this car parks itself at the harbor, we'll let ourselves out. There's probably a little convenience store nearby. We can run over there and buy a couple of cheap cell phones; Rahulla did a real number on our smartphones. Then, we'll call the police and have someone come over here and look at the car. Maybe this Raul character left some kind of electronic clues about who he is or where he is. We also get on that tour boat – with the spy bird – and go to the island. We need to make sure the tour guides don't see us at all, because they're probably in on the whole thing, too. Once we think we've found Raul, we can call the police again and tell them."

"Okay," said Leah, letting out a breath and sounding a bit calmer than before. "I think we'll have to split up. Rachel and I will stay by the car, while I call the police and have them take a look at it. You take the boys and the bird to the island. But the three of you absolutely need to stick together. Nobody gets separated, you hear?"

"That's not fair, Imma!" exclaimed Rachel. "I want to go on the boat!"

"Rachel," explained Leah patiently, "I want you to stay here with Imma while I call the police. Some bad men did something to our car. I promise I'll take you on another boat ride this summer."

For much of the drive, Rachel complained about how unfair it was, about how she never got to do any of the fun stuff, and about how the boys always got to do everything. Yosef took the Spy Squawker off of Yaakov's lap and began to examine it, ignoring his sister. Yaakov just sat quietly, resolving not to argue with Rachel over this one, because too much was at stake. Eventually, Rachel gave up her fight.

As their mysterious captor had predicted, the family SUV eventually made it to Ventura and parked itself neatly in a marked parking space at the harbor. It was 1:30 in the afternoon. Following the typical Southern California weather pattern, the morning cloud cover had given way to a hazy sunshine. Light crowds of people strolled by, and scattered beachgoers dotted the area, all of them oblivious to the Peretz family's predicament. The vehicle's doors unlocked themselves immediately after it had parked. As the five Peretzes exited their SUV, Yehuda and Leah briefly tested their smartphones again, with no luck.

After closing their vehicle's doors, Yehuda took the unmarked white envelope from under its windshield and opened it. He withdrew a bunch of little white tickets with imprinted bar codes and examined them briefly.

"Perfect timing," he announced. "We have half an hour until our boat boards at that dock." Then he pointed to an empty dock located to his left. "The boat's called *Pacific Dreamer.*"

I'd like to wake up from this bad dream, thought Yaakov.

"Fine," said Leah. "I spotted a 7-Eleven not far from here. Let's hurry up and get the new phones."

The five of them turned around and headed into Ventura Harbor Village, all walking at a brisk pace. They quickly found and entered the convenience store. Yehuda hurriedly told the clerk that he needed two cheap cell phones, and deflected all of the expected questions regarding activation, service plans, unlimited family texting, and other "conveniences." Finally, the purchase was complete, and the family walked out of the store with two simple black devices. Yehuda and Leah exchanged numbers as they rushed back to the harbor with their children. On the way, they quickly tested their phones by calling each other. They both sighed with relief upon finding their new phones to work.

"Less than ten minutes to go," said Yehuda, when they had returned to their parking space. He then turned to his sons. "Come on, boys."

"Good bye, guys," said Leah, with a wave. "Stay together, stay safe, and keep your eyes and ears open."

"We will," called Yaakov and Yosef, as they turned and left the parking lot.

"Welcome to Sailing Saway's Island Voyages," came the announcement several moments later, while Yaakov and Yosef stood on the crowded dock with their father. "We are now boarding the *Pacific Dreamer* for our 2:30 excursion to Anacapa Island. I'm your trusty tour guide, Leroy Caramel. Please present your tickets as you board. Then find your seats, sit back and get ready to enjoy the ocean breeze as we saaaaiiiiiilll…Saway!"

While they walked onto the boat, Yaakov heard a corny jingle from the little ship's loudspeakers, a repetitive tune with the words, "Come sail Saway with me," playing over and over again. Most of the other tourists seemed equally lighthearted and silly. Nothing about any of them seemed out of the ordinary. Leroy Caramel was a tall, broad-shouldered man who stood on the deck and greeted every passenger with a plastic grin as he or she boarded. Yehuda and his sons found their seats, and the ship soon left the harbor.

Their voyage to the island was rather peaceful. The

Pacific Dreamer sailed over twenty-one miles of blue ocean. Seagulls flew overhead, and some passengers occasionally pointed to various spots where they claimed that they had just caught glimpses of whales or dolphins. Others sat back or casually strolled around the ship, enjoying the mild breezes and panoramic views of the sea and the California coast. Yehuda and Yosef chatted about the surrounding scenes, while Yaakov sat and worried. He tried to calm himself by remembering his family's plan: to survey the island using the Spy Squawker, call the authorities if they saw anything funny, and then to turn around and head home. However, it was hard to shake the feeling that he was sailing straight into harm's way. He couldn't get Sabba Tzadok off of his mind, either.

The ship eventually arrived at a boat dock attached to the island. Another announcement soon came over the speaker system: "Here we are at Anacapa Island. Enjoy the rest of your afternoon here, folks. For those of you who can make it, we have a return voyage to Ventura Harbor scheduled to depart at 5:30. Thank you for joining us, and remember: when it's time to sail, do it the Saway way!"

Yaakov, Yosef and their father got up and began to walk to the dock, along with the crowd of other passengers. Yehuda led the way, staring straight ahead while walking quickly. When they were close to the dock, a tall and obese man in a pink polo shirt suddenly bumped into Yaakov.

"Oops," grunted the large man. "My mistake."

Leroy Caramel stood near the passenger gangplank that connected the ship to the dock. "Keep it moving, everyone," he announced over a megaphone.

The steady stream of departing passengers soon became a blur, and Yaakov could barely see his father and brother over their heads. He thought he caught a glimpse of them both stepping onto the dock.

"Hey, buddy," asked another burly man, who stood behind Yaakov, "you want to hurry it up?"

"Now, just a minute, here," replied the pink-shirted man. He bent down to tie his shoe, in no obvious hurry. Yaakov was now sandwiched between the two bickering strangers.

Suddenly, he felt a hand gripping his right shoulder. "Hey, what are you doing?" Yaakov asked, turning his head to the right.

Another hand shoved a foul-smelling red bandana over his nose and mouth, and the burly stranger's voice whispered into his ear: "I'll lock ya!"

"What?!" Yaakov tried to scream through the rag now covering his mouth.

"Let's throw him down into the secret deck with the old guy," said a voice that sounded just like the burly stranger.

The last thing that Yaakov heard was the pink-shirted man's voice. "Nah, Rahulla said the observation deck. He won't get out."

Then, everything turned to black.

4 A NOT-SO-SECRET MEETING

Yaakov awoke in an unfamiliar little room. He was sitting on a wooden chair placed against one wall. Looking around, he saw some life vests hanging from hooks on another wall. A beam of sunlight streamed into the room through a small round window to his left. Directly opposite him was a white door with a handle. It took a few seconds for him to remember what had happened to him and to figure out where he was. He seemed to be in some kind of storage room on the *Pacific Dreamer*. In various places throughout the room, there were wooden crates, probably containing sailing and fishing equipment.

Once Yaakov realized what had happened to him, he began to panic. He felt his heart start to race within him, and he began to sweat. Then, he stopped himself. *No*, he thought, *I can't let the pirates win. They've already taken Sabba Tzadok prisoner, but they can't have me.* He closed his eyes for several moments, breathed deeply, and calmed himself down. Next, he whispered a brief prayer for help. Finally, he opened his eyes and began to plot an escape plan. *Look at the bright side*, he told himself. *At least Rahulla's gang of pirates didn't tie me to this chair. What fools!* He stood up, walked across the room and tried to open the door. It was locked. *Okay, they're not that foolish.*

His next idea was to check the window. It had no handle. He looked through the glass, and saw several seagulls flying over the dock that he recognized at Anacapa Island. He also saw that there was no easy way to reach that dock from this floor of the ship; it was a steep vertical drop down to the bay, where shallow water and rocks would await him if he could jump. Yaakov began to pace the room, searching for any additional exits or any items that he could use to escape. He began trying to open some of the crates, but each box's lid was fastened tightly.

After about two minutes, Yaakov heard a "tap" at the window. He forgot about the crates and ran to the window, to be pleasantly surprised by what he saw. The Spy Squawker flew rapidly towards the window and bumped into it. Then, it backed up several inches, turned to its left, and flew in a small circle until it faced the window again. Once more, the toy bird raced toward the window, crashed into the glass, and backed up for another pass. Yaakov immediately understood what was happening. Someone in his family, probably Yosef, was using their new gadget to search for him, and had just found him!

On the phony parrot's next approach, Yaakov stared directly at it and mouthed, "Get me out of here! Quick!"

The bird continued its pattern of circling tightly in the air and then rushing at the window. It was clear to

Yaakov that Yosef intended to continue using the toy parrot to smash the glass until Yaakov could escape. While Yosef continued trying break the window, Yaakov turned around and started shoving a large and heavy crate toward the door. He soon managed to barricade it.

Meanwhile, the Spy Squawker continued its repeated crashes into the window. Finally, it managed to crack the glass. Yaakov felt excited for a brief moment, and then began to worry again. The only way out of this trap was down.

Remember that stunt pilot from the airshow, he thought. *Forget about what happens next. I've made up my mind. Now I'll do whatever I need to do.*

There was no choice. Yaakov had no desire to remain a captive. Nor did he think it smart to plummet into shallow water, only to be crushed by the rocks that lay closely beneath its surface. While the Spy Squawker repeatedly pounded the glass window, Yaakov grabbed a life vest from the wall and put it on. As soon as he did so, the Spy Squawker hit the windowpane for the last time. With a loud crashing sound, the window glass shattered into thousands of tiny fragments. The Spy Squawker briefly flew into the room, and then turned around and flew outside through the hole that it had just made.

"What was that?" shouted a distant voice. Then, there were footsteps.

Yaakov had no time to waste. Carefully, he brushed aside the few pieces of glass that remained lodged in the edges of the round window frame and took a look down. It was a long descent to that salty ocean water, and Yaakov felt a sinking sensation in the pit of his stomach. Although he harbored a secret fear of heights, the thought of being captured again was even worse. His captors would surely do a better job of trapping him the second time, if given a chance.

The footsteps grew louder. Yaakov pulled his *yarmulke* off his head and shoved it into his pocket. Then, he grabbed the edge of the window and hoisted himself upward. He stuck his left foot outside, lifted his right foot to the window, and jumped.

Warm coastal summer air rushed past him as he accelerated toward the blue water below. That sinking feeling returned as he thought about what he had just done. In a split second, it was replaced with the thrill of escape and victory. With the ocean surface rapidly approaching, Yaakov took a deep breath and held it. A split second later, he hit the water with a loud splash. He was free!

He sank for a couple of seconds and then floated back up to the water's surface. His eyes and nostrils began to sting from the salt in the ocean water. When he lifted his head from the water and looked toward the nearby rocky shore of the island, he saw his father and brother standing near the water's edge. Both of them called to Yaakov and made arm motions that beckoned him to approach. Yosef was holding the Spy Squawker in one hand and its remote control in the other. Yaakov saw his backpack by his father's feet. He immediately unstrapped the life vest and removed it, letting it float. Next, he took off his shoes and carried them, to lighten the load on his feet. Then, he began to swim toward his father and brother, moving his arms and legs with all his might, knowing that there was little time before his escape was discovered.

"Come on, Yaakov! Hurry!" called Yehuda from the shore. "Hurry up!"

Almost immediately, he heard a familiar and upsetting voice. "Get back here, kid!" thundered Pink Shirt, the sinister stranger who had "accidentally" bumped into him on the deck of the *Pacific Dreamer*. "Now!"

Yaakov resisted the urge to turn around and look for the source of that voice. He simply kept swimming for life, pounding his limbs into the water with every ounce of strength that he could muster and drawing himself closer to the shore with every passing moment. As he swam to the island, he refused to imagine who might be pursuing him at that moment or how close those pursuers might be. Finally, after what seemed an eternity, he felt his father's powerful, loving arms pulling him out of the water and embracing him.

"You made it!" said Yosef, as soon as Yaakov had stepped onto the shore. "Great swimming, Yaakov!"

"Thanks for busting me out of there, Yosef," he replied. "I really owe you one."

"Thank goodness you're all right!" exclaimed Yehuda as he let go of his soaked son. He continued speaking quickly. "We were following the group for a little while, waiting for Captain Saway to head off on his own, before we realized you were missing. Imma's panicked, and-"

"Later, Abba," interrupted Yaakov, pointing to the nearby dock. "He's coming!"

Now, Yaakov's angry-looking captor was approaching, running down the bridge that connected the boat to the shore. He was clearly a lot larger than Yaakov's father. In his left hand, he carried a crowbar, which he waved in a threatening manner while he approached Yehuda Peretz and his two sons. Fortunately, Pink Shirt didn't seem very nimble.

"Let's run, boys!" yelled Yehuda. He and the boys turned and began to race away from the shore. For a split second, Yaakov felt a rush of air by his right ear, and thought that he heard something whiz past him. He turned his head and instantly spotted the ninja star that had just been thrown at him. It was now lodged firmly in a rock wall, its razor-sharp blades glistening in the sun.

The Pink Ninja's on the loose! thought Yaakov, ridiculously, for a brief instant.

Yehuda continued speaking in a loud whisper, as he and the two boys continued to outrun their pursuer. "We'll need to contact the authorities soon about that boat tour. But right now, our best bet is to find the tour group. We'll blend in with the crowd, and that thug will be outnumbered."

"They took that trail, Abba," said Yosef. He pointed to a sandy trail that seemed to disappear over a little hill. "I saw them with the Spy Squawker."

"Lead the way, Yosef," answered Yehuda.

The three of them headed toward the trail. Yaakov did not want to waste a moment putting on his wet shoes. The trail's even surface provided him with some relief from the stones that had been piercing his aching feet until then. They passed many flowery meadows, rocks and observation points that would have been nice to admire on a normal family picnic. Though Yaakov ignored most of the tiny island's scenery, he tried to remember a few specific landmarks, in case he got separated from his father and brother again. Eventually, the sounds of the Pink Ninja's footsteps grew more distant. Yehuda and his boys soon slowed down to a fast walk.

Soon, Yosef stopped walking and pointed. "Abba, I think they're behind those bushes."

"You mean the guys from the boat?" asked Yehuda, in a low voice.

"No," answered Yosef, "the tourists. That's where they were hanging around a few minutes ago, when I spotted them with the Spy Squawker. They're probably still resting over there."

Yehuda smiled. "Then let's go join the fun."

Nobody in the tour group seemed to notice the three sweaty, out-of-breath individuals who soon emerged from the shrubbery: a man with a wet boy who carried his shoes and a dry boy who held onto a remote-controlled parrot. They were now a bit far from the shore at which the *Pacific Dreamer* had landed. Yaakov sat on the ground for a moment and put on his shoes. Although he understood that Rahulla's overgrown henchman was still after them, he also needed a rest. He figured that he was safe in this crowd, and recognized some of the individual tourists whom he had seen on the ship. Now, many of them sat on large boulders, casually sipping water from plastic bottles and admiring the magnificent views. Others milled around, chatting about trivial matters or taking pictures of flowers.

Are all of these passengers a bunch of criminals, Yaakov wondered, *or has Rahulla Allijabulla planted only a couple of them in the crowd in order to trick us?*

Yehuda found Leroy Caramel discussing the island's features with a couple and explaining some of the things that they saw. He approached the tour guide, along with Yaakov and Yosef.

"Excuse me, Leroy," said Yehuda, getting Leroy's attention.

Leroy turned to Yehuda with a wide grin. He seemed to be a very smiley guy. "Yes, sir," he answered.

"We're looking for Captain Saway," continued Yehuda. "We have to talk to him about something."

"Oh, I'd hate to disturb Captain Saway right now," responded Leroy, still smiling. "He's resting. He's been real busy lately."

"It's about something really important," said Yehuda.

"Hmmm...." answered Leroy, pausing for a few seconds. "Can I give him a message?"

"I'm afraid it's very urgent. We need to see him right away."

"Okay," said Leroy. "I'll tell you what." He turned to the couple for moment and excused himself, then led Yehuda and his sons several feet away from them. Pointing to a path in the dirt, Leroy continued speaking in a quiet voice: "Captain Saway likes to relax in the caves. I don't know what he does in them. Go and follow that trail toward the other side of the island. You'll see some little caves, and he's probably in one of them. Don't tell him that I sent you."

"Got it," replied Yehuda. "Thanks. Come on, boys."

The three of them set down the narrow, winding dirt path that seemed to lead nowhere. It was all unknown territory, but Yaakov now felt braver than when he had first arrived on the island. His father and brother were with him, and they had a Spy Squawker. What could go wrong?

Eventually, they found themselves atop a low hill,

overlooking a small area where several little caves led into the ground. The sun had now mostly dried Yaakov's hair, skin and clothing, but his shoes were still wet. Yaakov suddenly realized something awful and stopped walking.

"Uh-oh," he said.

Yehuda and Yosef both stopped. "What's wrong?" asked Yehuda, turning to face him.

"I've just left a whole trail of muddy footprints on the ground," he answered, sheepishly, pointing to the footsteps behind him.

"No problem," said Yehuda. "You're a big boy, but I can still carry you. I'll pick you up and take you behind that rock." He pointed to a large nearby boulder. "We'll hide out there and launch the Spy Squawker, and we can use that to search for Captain Saway." Yehuda lifted Yaakov and held him in both arms. "Come, Yosef."

Yosef ran to the boulder and squatted behind it, and was followed immediately by his father and brother. "Spy Squawker ready for takeoff," he announced in a quiet voice.

He quickly turned on the toy bird and tapped the "LAUNCH" button located on the controller's display screen. The bird flew into the air. Yosef steered it toward the caves below them, while the three of them stared at the screen. Yosef carefully navigated the bird toward one of the caves. It swooped close to the entrance, and then climbed upwards again.

"I think I saw someone in there," said Yaakov.

"I think you're right," replied Yosef. "Let's take another look." He steered the bird back toward the cave. The display showed a dim image of a man standing near a cave wall, hunched over, his face hidden by shadows. This image grew larger as the bird flew closer to the cave.

"Why don't we land it on a rock or something, and just watch them?" asked Yaakov.

"Good idea," answered Yehuda. "Yosef, please see if you can get the bird to land somewhere."

"I'm doing that," he replied.

Yosef steered the Spy Squawker away from the cave, and the three of them watched as the cave grew more distant. Staring at the display, Yosef navigated the bird to the branch of a short nearby tree. From there, the cave was visible. Yosef zoomed the view of the cave until the display showed more detail. Then, he tapped the display's "RECORD" button. From their hiding place, the Peretzes watched and recorded a mystifying scene unfold.

The shadowy figure in the cave remained hunched over, and soon started digging into the sand with his bare hands. Very little sunlight entered this cave, so it was difficult to see the individual's face. After a few moments, another man entered the cave and approached the first man.

The hunched figure looked up for a moment and greeted his guest. "What took you so long? That drone flyover never happened. I kept looking up in the sky for Goleta Gadgets Express. I waited and waited for you to drop in. I even found a place to hide your parachute. How'd you finally get here, anyway?" he asked.

"Yeah," replied the guest, "the drone never showed up, all right. Good crooks are hard to find these days. Remember that sloppy little kid I told you about? Some bully. He couldn't keep his fool trap shut, and got caught. And guess who turned him in? That same meddling boy from Djerba! What a weird family that kid has. They play with pet rodents and bring them on trips. Anyway, don't worry about the boy; I took care of him. Good thing I had a Plan B."

Yaakov shuddered when he heard those words. Back on the boat, his kidnappers had mentioned where Rahulla had told them to lock up Sabba Tzadok, and this strange man in the cave had just admitted responsibility. He must be Rahulla Allijabulla!

"What did you pull this time?" asked the shadowy hunchback.

"I've got connections," answered Rahulla. "Today I'm Captain Saway of the *Pacific Dreamer*. The kid's stuck on the boat, and the old guy's locked up, too. So they won't be bothering us."

"Wow," replied the hunchback, "you're the best identity thief I've ever met."

"Yeah, yeah, yeah." answered Rahulla. "Now what are you looking for?"

"My tablet," said the hunchback. "It's buried in here somewhere."

"Here, let me help you," offered Rahulla. He pulled a little object out of his pocket and pushed a button. A bright LED lamp now lit up the cave, and the other man's face was now visible on the Spy Squawker's display. Yaakov gasped. The other man was Bobby the Brute! Quickly, Yaakov tapped the screen's "SNAPSHOT" button to take a still photo of the two men. With a few more taps, he sent the picture to his parents' smartphones, hoping that they would soon work again.

Bobby gruffly thanked Rahulla for the light, and

continued digging in the sand. Soon, he managed to uncover a rolled-up flexible tablet computer that had been buried in the sand. He pulled it out of the ground, unrolled it and turned it on. "I managed to send myself an email from Djerba. Look at this."

The two men looked at the Bobby's tablet.

"We've got to see what's on that screen," whispered Yaakov to Yosef. "Can you move the bird around just a bit?"

"I think so," answered Yosef. "I'm getting really good at this." He used the remote control to maneuver the bird's position slowly and quietly. Soon, Bobby the Brute's tablet came into view, and his screen was fairly clear to Yaakov, Yosef and their father.

"Whoa!" said Rahulla. "Where'd you take these pictures?"

"Israel," answered Bobby. "I snooped around there a little on my way to Djerba. That's Timna Valley Park. You see all that digging equipment? They're getting ready to dig up King Solomon's mines, from ancient times."

"Are you pulling my leg?" asked Rahulla, sounding a little bit upset. "I'm warning you! I'm the one who found you and made you who you are today. You were just Robert A. Montrose, laid-off electronics engineer in Van Nuys. Now look at you: Bobby the Brute, international pirate. You want to go back to that Tunisian prison? I don't think so. The food here's a lot better."

"Tell me about it. Every night they fed us this wicked mushroom soup. Phew! It was horrible. I'll never forgive them for that. The cook over there was a real jerk and a half."

"You see?" asked Rahulla. "Look how well you're doing now. You need me, so don't waste my time with nonsense."

"Yeah," retorted Bobby, "look how much better I'm doing now. That apartment on Oxnard Boulevard was a real dump. This cave's far more elegant. Anyway, I'm not pulling your leg, Rahulla. You know how hard it is to hack a weather report with a smartphone? I didn't do that for nothing. I'm really showing you the site of King Solomon's copper mines. The Israelis found them about ten, twelve years ago. Now, they're pretty sure there's something valuable still under the ground there. On Thursday morning, they're gonna dig more holes and mine the place for national treasure, like artifacts and precious metals, unless..."

"Unless what?" asked Rahulla, in a condescending tone.

"Unless we get to it first," answered Bobby.

"Who's 'we'?"

Bobby the Brute stammered a bit. "Y-you, me, the other pirates. I figure it'll be our next heist. They'll want a good one after that fiasco in Santa Barbara. Now look closely. We don't have a lot of time. A few explosions will create a distraction and give us plenty of time to rob some good loot. They'll have to clear everybody out of the park. That's when we move in and grab whatever ancient relics we can find. I've already hidden some plastic explosives in the park. They're set up for the greatest possible distraction. Of course we wear gloves, and all that. You've got the funds, so we can leave right away."

Although Yaakov couldn't see the screen very clearly, and had no idea where Bobby had planned to place his bombs, he knew that this recorded confession was priceless.

"You know what?" asked Rahulla. "I like the way you think, Bobby. But I figure I can actually pull off this one as a solo operation. I don't think I'll need to hire any pirates this time around. Anyway, pirates are getting a little…passé. Don't you agree?"

"What if I dressed up as a wizard this time, instead?" Bobby the Brute now sounded desperate. "I could carry a stink bomb under my robe and-"

"Forget it, Robert. Your time has come and gone. The Rahulla Collections enterprise will be a one-man operation from now on, and that one man is me. Great idea about King Solomon's ancient treasures, though. But those time bombs really need to go off at night, in my humble opinion. I can turn on some digging equipment myself. So, let's say I want to set them for Wednesday night. How would I do that?"

"You wouldn't," answered Bobby. "You can't reset them at all without their detonator, which I threw together using my car-door opener."

"That little piece of junk from your old Toyota?"

"Yeah," replied Bobby, "that little piece of junk. That's also hidden in the Nature Reserve, in just the right spot. And even if you do find it, you'll be lost without the passcode. That's stored on a fob that I buried in the Red Sea by Coral Beach, off the coast of Eilat. It's protected by a bunch of jellborgs that I stole from a Japanese cargo ship."

Yaakov had no idea what a "fob" was, but it sounded dangerous.

"A bunch of *what?*" asked Rahulla.

"Jellborgs," replied Bobby, smugly. "Weaponized

robotic jellyfish. They're too dangerous to sell to the public, so you won't find them in any stores or online. If you really want to manage this heist at all, I'd suggest you bring me along."

"Nah," said Rahulla, "I think Van Nuys is a better fit for you. I can't have a loose cannon like you running around the world and getting caught, like you did last time. Just tell me where your detonator is, and I'll be on my way."

"What?" yelled Bobby, sounding shocked. "After all I've done for you? Come on, Rahulla. You need me. "

"You heard what I said, Bobby. Tell me where the bombs are, and the detonator, or I can get Vinnie to…coax you."

"Come on, Rahulla," pleaded Bobby the Brute, "don't I at least get my finder's fee? You promised! What I've just told you is solid gold. And after all I've done for you, you can't double-cross me like that!"

"I just did," answered Rahulla, coldly. "But you know what? I'm in a merciful mood today. I'll call off Vinnie, and you'll soon be rewarded for your efforts with a free trip back to Djerba. You've told me all I need to know. Enjoy your mushroom soup."

Yaakov suddenly heard a gruff voice behind him. "Well, well, there you are! My guest! Now what were you thinking, leaving through the window like that, without even saying goodbye?"

Yaakov slowly stood up and turned around, to find himself face-to-face with the Pink Ninja. His father and brother stood and faced the rotund man, as well.

"Let me see what you've got there," continued the kidnapper, pointing to the Spy Squawker's controller.

"You want it?" asked Yaakov, defiantly. "Okay."

He instantly snatched the controller from Yosef and hurled it to his left with all his might. Then, he bolted to his right, dashing away from the Pink Ninja at top speed, while his former captor went scrambling for the device. Yaakov had no idea where the controller had landed, and he didn't care. His father and brother followed him closely. The three of them sprinted from the scene as quickly as their exhausted legs allowed them to run.

5 THE RESCUE

While he ran across the island with his father and brother, Yaakov hurriedly told them about his worries concerning Sabba Tzadok. "We have to get back on that boat right away. They've got Sabba Tzadok trapped down there, and now that Rahulla's had his little meeting, there's no telling what they'll do to him!"

Without responding, Yehuda and Yosef accompanied Yaakov all the way back to the walkway that connected the *Pacific Dreamer* to the dock. Yaakov silently grabbed his backpack from his father's hands and put it on. The three of them then ran onto the *Pacific Dreamer* and began to search it for their missing friend. Yaakov headed straight for the staircase that led to the vessel's lower levels, while the other two Peretzes searched the upper decks.

Immediately on descending the stairs, Yaakov noticed a small open trap door on the floor across from him. He sprang across the floor in an instant, and peered into the little chamber exposed by the little open door. The chamber was empty at that moment, yet seemed large enough to hold one person in an uncomfortable position.

Suddenly, Yaakov heard footsteps moving across the deck above him. He dashed over to the staircase and leapt up the steps as quickly as he could. As he reached the middle deck, he realized that he was not a moment too soon. The same thug who had grabbed Yaakov from behind earlier that day was now walking toward the edge of the boat, carrying an unconscious Sabba Tzadok over his right shoulder.

Yaakov shuddered with fright for a split second, and then pushed that fright out of his mind. Now was not a time to be afraid. Sabba Tzadok was in trouble, and Yaakov had to perform a *mitzvah*, a Divine commandment from the Torah, by saving the elderly man's life. *Concentrate on what I'm doing right now*, he told himself, *and forget everything else.*

Quickly as lightning, Yaakov raced across the deck, pulled his fishing rod out of his backpack, aimed it in the thug's direction, and flicked a little switch on the rod's handle. The rod extended to its full length, its hook dangling several inches from the would-be murderer's left eye.

I'm not scared of this guy, Yaakov thought, as the criminal's expression changed from bored nastiness to shock and awe. Though he held Sabba Tzadok's limp body dangerously close to the boat's railing, the thug froze in his tracks for a brief moment.

Then, he opened his mouth. "Get that thing away from me, kid! You've got some nerve!"

"Put him down on the deck!" roared Yaakov. "Slowly!"

"Don't kid yourself, boy," snapped the thug, sounding arrogant. As he spoke, he visibly tightened his grip on Sabba Tzadok. "Just turn around, walk away, and pretend you didn't see nuthin'."

Yaakov inched the fishing hook slightly closer to the thug's face. *Don't give in*, he told himself. *This guy will fold if I just keep at it.* His next command came out of his mouth slowly and clearly. "Put the man down, right now, or you're going to lose an eye."

Tzadok Sapir's captor stood in place and looked at Yaakov silently for several seconds, before finally lowering the elderly man and placing him gently onto the deck of the *Pacific Dreamer*.

"Now step away from him," Yaakov commanded. He couldn't believe his own newfound courage and authority. However, he wasn't sure what order to give next, or how long this newfound power over an adult criminal would last.

Yehuda and Yosef answered those questions for him. They suddenly appeared, as if from nowhere, leaping at the brute from behind and tackling him to the deck. Yaakov instantly jumped into action once more. He grabbed a spool of fishing wire from his backpack and tied together the hands of Sabba Tzadok's bewildered captor, behind his back, while Yehuda and Yosef kept the man pinned down. Next, Yaakov tied together the man's feet. Finally, with Yehuda pressing the thug's body to the deck, the Peretz brothers wrapped several loops of fishing wire around his arms.

As soon as they were finished tying up the assailant, Yehuda's phone rang.

"Hello, Leah," Yehuda answered his phone, squatting with knee on the deck and one knee pressing down on the tied-up criminal's back. He also pressed the man's back with his left arm, while holding the phone in his right hand. The thug squirmed and grunted incoherently while Yehuda spoke. Yaakov and Yosef sat on the deck throughout the conversation that followed.

Yaakov overheard his mother's worried voice from the other end. "Did you find Yaakov? What's going on right now? We haven't talked in a while."

Yehuda grinned triumphantly. "We've found him, Leah. He somehow got a little…separated from the group. But he's fine. We're all fine."

"Oh, good." Leah sounded relieved. "So…what's happening? What happened to Sabba Tzadok?"

As if on cue, Tzadok Sapir opened his eyes, rubbed them briefly and sat up. "It's the Peretz family!" he greeted Yehuda and his sons, who looked at Tzadok in silence as he spoke to them. "What's going on? How did I get here?"

Leah's voice came from the phone. "Yehuda? Are you still there? Hello?"

"Leah?" he replied. Tzadok's would-be murderer writhed on the ground, obviously trying to get away, while Yehuda spoke. "Sorry. Yes, he's with us. Everything's fine. We've been a little busy for the past couple of hours. And, boy, do we have a lot to tell you! Can I save it for the ride home?"

"Sure. The car's working again, and Rachel and I have a pretty exciting tale of our own."

The boys' parents agreed to share stories on the way home, and then ended their conversation. Leroy Caramel's voice was soon heard, approaching, as he led his tour group back onto the *Pacific Dreamer*. Their chattering voices gave Yaakov a mild comfort. *Time to wrap things up*, he thought.

"Mr. Caramel!" called Yaakov. "Over here!"

"Coming!" came Leroy's baritone voice in reply.

Leroy Caramel appeared on the scene about ten seconds later, and seemed instantly shocked by what he saw. He spent a moment or two absorbing the scene in front of him, and then wondered aloud, "What in the *world* is going on over here?"

"These crazy passengers knocked me down and tied me up! Just like that, for no reason!" barked the thug, still squirming to escape from Yehuda's grip.

"That's a lie!" shouted Yaakov, before Leroy could answer. "We caught this man trying to throw another man overboard and drown him!" He pointed to Sabba Tzadok. "He's right there. I stopped this guy from doing it."

Leroy gave the thug a hard look. "Is that true, Vinnie?"

Vinnie the thug began to sweat. "Leroy, you know I never lie to you," he sputtered.

"Somehow, I'm not so sure I believe that," answered Leroy, coolly. "You've been acting kind of funny lately."

"Leroy," stammered Vinnie, "come on. We're old pals. You've gotta believe me."

"Hey, what's all the hubbub?" interrupted the familiar voice of Captain Saway. Yaakov looked up and saw him standing next to Leroy Caramel. "And what are you doing down there, Vinnie?"

"These guys jumped me, Captain! I was just trying to do what you said."

"What?" Captain Saway looked mildly surprised.

Yaakov quickly stood up and peered down at Vinnie. "All four of you are up to something really bad. You, this man on the floor, that guy with the pink shirt, and you, Rahulla." He looked straight at Captain Saway before adding those last three words.

Captain Saway faced Yaakov and replied, without missing a beat. "Uh...the name is Saway," he said, contemptuously. "Montgomery Saway, or *Captain* Saway to you, my young friend. Anyway, let's get this cleared up." He looked over his shoulder for a moment. "Bruce! Hey, Bruce, we need you over here."

"Coming, Captain!" called the man whom Yaakov had privately named the Pink Ninja. He came from around a corner and lumbered over to Captain Saway. "What can I do for you, Cap?"

Tzadok Sapir stood up and pointed at Bruce, the Pink Ninja. "That's him. That's the man who grabbed me when I showed up at the dock. He shoved a smelly rag into my face. The next thing I knew, I was on this boat."

"And Vinnie did the same thing to me!" exclaimed Yaakov.

"Well, that's just awful," said Captain Saway, addressing the Peretzes and Tzadok with fake-sounding sympathy. "I'm really disappointed about all the things that I'm hearing. So sorry your experience on Sailing Saway's Island Voyages wasn't the very best it could be. We'll have to alert the authorities ASAP." Then, he turned to Leroy. "Leroy, why don't you keep an eye on these two...*former*...employees, while we head back to Ventura?"

"With pleasure," answered Leroy Caramel.

"And let's get this ship sailing! Sailing Saway!"

exclaimed Captain Saway. He then began walking to another part of the vessel.

Yaakov spoke to Captain Saway as he passed him. "I know what you're up to, Rahulla. You're not gonna get away with it."

Captain Saway paused for a moment and gave Yaakov one of the meanest looks that he had ever seen from an adult. "You're dreaming, kid."

On the way back to Ventura Harbor, the Peretzes had plenty of time to discuss their experiences with Sabba Tzadok. Rahulla's complicated plot was now crystal clear to Yaakov, and the others listened intently while he explained everything.

Back on Djerba, several weeks earlier, Bobby the Brute had actually managed to send Rahulla Allijabulla a communication, right before being captured. It was a coded message hidden within a weather broadcast. The message was an invitation to meet him in the pirates' former hideout, their little cave on Anacapa Island. Bobby expected Rahulla to get the hint that he had something big in store for Rahulla, if only Rahulla would get him out of prison.

Rahulla managed to use his connections and bribery to get Bobby the Brute released. At the same time, he wanted to be sure that the same people who had ruined his earlier plans to steal Djerba's ancient Torah scroll would be unable to stop this next crime. To do so, he busted the other pirates out of jail as well, and used Plavarto to bug Yaakov in order to keep track of his movements. The pirates could also provide convenient help in carrying out several crimes along the way.

Since he was a wanted man, Rahulla couldn't just travel around like an ordinary person; he had to use an unusual method to transport himself to Anacapa Island. His plan was to sneak onto a drone aircraft headed from Van Nuys to Goleta, and to parachute onto the island eventually. Plavarto had been expected to deliver the necessary parachute to Powder-keg Fred the pirate, who would place onto the plane for Rahulla. Unfortunately for Rahulla, Yaakov ruined that plan by turning in Plavarto to the LAPD.

Rahulla needed an alternate plan, a "Plan B." Being a master of disguise and deception, he impersonated Captain Saway and took command of his ship. He also had both Tzadok Sapir and Yaakov kidnapped in order to make certain that they stayed out of the way. By escaping from his kidnappers, Yaakov managed to discover Bobby the Brute's big plot.

"It's a real danger, and I think Rahulla plans on following through with it," said Tzadok Sapir, after Yaakov had finished his explanation. "He needs to be stopped."

"But how?" asked Yosef, glaring at Yaakov. "We lost all the evidence. No police anywhere will believe us."

"Then we'll have to do it ourselves," said Yaakov, defensively.

"Yaakov, I think we're done adventuring for a while," said his father. "You told a good story, but we're not even really sure that the person we saw in that cave was really Rahulla Allijabulla. Let's just head back to Los Angeles as soon we can, and forget about the whole thing. There's still a little time to fish in the lake before dark."

6 COPPER MINES AND JELLYFISH

The pickles were delicious. Yaakov sat on a soft, leathery seat, wordlessly chomping on the crunchy, spicy appetizers spread in front of him, while the adults conversed. It was getting late, but the crowd at Babylon Grill restaurant in Sherman Oaks showed no signs of leaving. Both Yosef and Rachel slumbered in the adjacent seats, while Yaakov munched on cooked Middle-Eastern style goodies.

His parents had quickly set up a meeting that night with Tzadok Sapir and his grandson, Aharon, who had flown from Santa Barbara to Los Angeles a short while earlier in his private jet. They were also joined by Dilip Sitoop, the Peretz Family's trusty robot dealer. Although Yaakov would have preferred a good night's rest after all that had happened that day, he knew that tonight's meeting was too important to ignore. So, he forced himself to stay awake and to pay attention while the adults discussed the odd events that had recently taken place. As Yaakov bit into his second Moroccan cigar, his mother began to tell her story.

"Right after sending you guys off on your island tour, I used my new phone to call Slersky Labs. They're one of the big computer security companies. I told them that somebody had taken control of our car and driven us to a faraway destination against our will. Of course, I also told them about the threats against Sabba Tzadok and us. So the people at Slersky got in touch with both the L.A. and Ventura Police Departments, and worked with them to find out who was responsible." As Leah had explained to the kids earlier that day, the people who had kidnapped them in their own vehicle were guilty of a cybercrime. "Cybercrime" is crime committed through a computer network. All driverless cars were controlled by computers in their engines, and all of those computers were connected to each other through a massive network.

Leah continued: "By examining our engine and Yehuda's old phone, the authorities were able to track down the source of that break-in to our vehicle. Guess who did it?"

"Who?" asked Aharon, leaning forward in his seat, clearly fascinated by the tale.

"Pete Weasel."

Aharon's eyes widened. "Are you serious?"

Pete Weasel was the head of the band of pirates who had robbed the Sapir mansion earlier that summer.

"Yeah," answered Leah, "I'm serious. And now we know his real name. It's Pedro Jimenez. He was sharing a grungy apartment on Oxnard Street with the other six bums who robbed your home a few weeks ago. Pedro was their gang leader. They called themselves 'The

Pirates of Van Nuys.' When the police raided that apartment today and nabbed him, they forced him to identify that mysterious 'Raul' character who threatened Sabba Tzadok and us. So Pedro, or Pete Weasel, claimed that 'Raul' was just a fake name used by Rahulla Allijabulla."

Aharon's mouth dropped open. "Unbelievable."

"Indeed," replied Leah. "And that's not all. The Pirates of Van Nuys were all working for Rahulla Allijabulla. They'd been working for him all summer. When they weren't hanging out in a cave on Anacapa, that bunch of sloppy jerks all lived together in a dingy little apartment with ratty carpets and a smelly kitchen, along with some pretty hi-tech digital stuff. They arranged the hack on our car, the bug in my son's backpack and Rahulla's bizarre phone call." She leaned back in her chair and let out a sigh.

"But those guys are out of commission now," offered Yehuda.

"Right," replied Leah. "But remember that they weren't the only ones working for that Rahulla creep. He's a criminal mastermind. He hired a couple of other brutes to kidnap both Yaakov and Sabba Tzadok, just to make sure they stayed out of his way while he met with Bobby the Brute to plot their next heist. Now, those two thugs have been caught, too, but Rahulla keeps slipping away. He's used a lot of fake identities to sneak around and avoid capture. We think that one of those identities is Captain Saway, but we can't prove it."

"Until now," said Dilip Sitoop, who hadn't yet spoken. "His facial expression gave him away." All eyes were now on Dilip and the tablet computer that he held for the others to see.

The tablet showed the picture that Yaakov had taken on Friday afternoon using the Spy Squawker: Rahulla and Bobby the Brute discussing Bobby's latest plot. On top of Rahulla's image, mainly around his mouth, were numerous orange squiggles with little letters and numbers next to them. Also on the screen was a smaller version of another picture, a photo taken by Yaakov on Djerba several weeks earlier in front of the El-Ghriba synagogue. The picture from Djerba showed a man in a ski mask sitting behind the steering wheel of an old Lincoln Town Car. His face was almost entirely covered, except for his eyes and mouth. The driver's mouth was open in a grimace that showed obvious frustration. There were some curves, squiggles, numbers, and letters around the man's mouth in this picture, too.

Dilip pointed to a message that appeared in red text at the upper right-hand corner of the tablet's display: "Match Prob.: 98.83%." "Your suspect made a critical mistake, my friends," explained Dilip. "He opened his mouth for the cameras."

"So, let me get this straight," said Leah Peretz, looking directly at Dilip Sitoop. "You're saying there's no question that the guy on the island who claimed to be this...'Captain Saway' character really is the same person who drove that car to the El-Ghriba synagogue to meet Bobby the Brute a few weeks ago. Is that right?"

"Well," answered Dilip, "I'll put it this way. My facial recognition software gave us over a 98% match between the two pictures, almost 99%. Again, this would have been impossible if he had kept his mouth closed back there on Djerba. There would have been no way to match the pictures of the two men. But, fortunately, I was able to focus on his mouth, especially his teeth. So, yes, I'd say you're looking at the same person." Dilip put down the tablet and turned his attention to the plate of hummus in front of him.

"Whoa," said Leah, leaning back in her chair. Then, she faced Yaakov with a wry smile. "You see how important it is to keep your mouth shut?"

Yaakov chuckled a bit, still resting his right elbow on the table with his face in his hand as he continued his valiant fight against sleep.

"But this morning," continued Leah, "it was good that you opened your mouth and said something. You stopped some very bad people from doing some awful things."

"I'm not so sure they've been stopped yet," said Sabba Tzadok. "That Captain Saway character is still at large. We can't just let him be."

"Okay," said Yehuda, "so suppose Dilip's right, and the people in the two photos really are the same person, and that person's name is really Rahulla Allijabulla. And suppose he really meant it when he told Bobby the Brute he wanted to travel to Israel to set off some explosions and steal artifacts. What do you want from our lives? I mean, there's nothing we can do about it, anyway."

"I'm afraid that somebody has to do something," answered Tzadok Sapir. Yaakov paid him close attention. He knew that Sabba Tzadok was a very wise and learned man, who had educated his family on the Djerba Jewish community and its ancient Torah scroll earlier that summer. "First of all, even if there's little chance that this strange man will actually go and

73

endanger other people, we have to take his threat seriously. Secondly, think about which archaeological site he may be endangering and what kinds of artifacts it may contain.

"Timna Valley Park wasn't always a park. It's in the southern part of the Land of Israel, and it's where King Solomon once owned and operated many copper mines. For a long time, the archaeological record made it pretty clear that people did mine for copper there, and smelted it. The copper was generally combined with sand to make saws, but sometimes people used it for ornaments, too.

"Back in 2013, archaeologists made a major discovery there. That year, some excavations proved that those mines in the Timna Valley really dated to the time of King Solomon, and were not Egyptian property from 300 years earlier, as they had generally thought until then. You can't blame them for thinking so, because an ancient Egyptian temple was actually uncovered in the area at one time. Anyway, in 2013, a team of archaeologists dug up the site, and found all kinds of things from King Solomon's days. Besides hundreds of copper furnaces, they also discovered ceramics, clothing, foods like pistachios and grapes, ropes, and other items. It's possible that the Edomites, who were constantly at war with the Jewish people during Solomon's reign, first dug those mines.

"What's even more interesting is what this discovery tells us about archaeology itself: it doesn't always tell us the full story of what happened in the past. It can't. Think about what the mining and smelting operations revealed about life in ancient Israel during Solomon's era. There was an incredibly advanced society living there – thousands of people living in the desert, digging for copper – and yet nobody would have known about them if they had been involved in anything other than mining. Nobody but us, I mean, because of our Jewish tradition. But what would others have known about them? Nothing. The people lived in tents, which don't last very long, and wouldn't have left behind any buildings or monuments.

"So, it's important to realize that by robbing an archaeological dig, like the upcoming dig at King Solomon's mines, this character whom you witnessed yesterday afternoon would be erasing the evidence of an ancient people – they would vanish from history without a trace. True, he's just a thief, and there's no doubt that there are more discoveries waiting to be made in Timna Valley; he could probably make a pretty penny on the black market for stolen artifacts. You could say that his theft has nothing to do with us, but do you really want to just let this criminal go and erase a part of history? Hasn't enough of that been done already?"

Leah faced Sabba Tzadok and responded. "Mr. Sapir, thank you for that beautiful explanation. I'm really impressed by your knowledge and wisdom. And, you're right – to just sit back and let this Rahulla go to Israel and rob those artifacts would be a truly great loss. But, what else is there to do? We've already told the Israeli authorities, and they said they would increase security at the park. So, we did our job. There's nothing more to talk about."

"Well, my friends," offered Dilip, "I would have said the very same the same thing, except for all the clues that the pirate gave us. I'm not sure that any police force would act so quickly on those clues, which sound like nonsense. But you can certainly help them by gathering some hard evidence yourselves. Bobby the Brute gave himself away when he told Rahulla about his stolen jellborgs – you know, those weaponized robotic jellyfish that you heard him mention. That's how you'll help the authorities catch him – before anything happens."

Yaakov sat up straight at Dilip's mention of robotic jellyfish. Robots were his favorite hobby. He had played and tinkered with many of them over the years, and even built some. But he had never thought of throwing one of them into water. "What do you mean, Mr. Sitoop?"

"Here's what I mean, Yaakov," answered Dilip. "I'm surprised he was even able to pluck any of those things out of the water in the first place, without getting caught. The very first robotic jellyfish were developed a number of years ago for the U.S. Navy. Still, even though they're not a totally new invention, not very many people know much about them. Jellborgs were designed to do things like cleaning up oil spills, monitoring the ocean, that sort of thing. So, they've been dropped into various spots in the ocean waters all around the world.

"Now, there was Bobby the Brute, sailing on his way to Djerba, when he came across a few of these gadgets that looked like jellyfish floating in the water. Being an electronics engineer in his former life – I mean, before he decided to become a pirate – he must have been able to tell that they weren't real. And, he was probably pretty bored, too. I mean, how many raw fish can a guy eat while he's sailing on a little boat and looking at the same blue ocean water that just seems to stretch on forever? He must have disabled each jellyfish's tracking device right after grabbing it out of the water, so that nobody could follow him. Then, he probably just started tinkering with them. Who knows what kind of miniature electronic devices he carried with him on that little fishing boat of his?

"My guess is that Bobby started reprogramming a few robotic jellyfish to protect a little object by swarming around it and surrounding it from all sides, so that nobody can grab it."

"And how do those jellborgs prevent someone from stealing the controller?" asked Yaakov.

"Probably by zapping him with mild electric shocks to scare him off. Those would be the robotic version of a real jellyfish's sting."

Yaakov leaned toward Dilip, with his right elbow on the table in front of him and his chin in his hand. This situation was getting interesting. "So where do we come in?"

Dilip lowered his voice to a whisper. "I'll tell you," he said. "I've been working on my own variety of jellborgs. I doubt that they work exactly the same way as the military ones, because they're my own invention, and I've got nothing to do with militaries.

"Basically, the robotic jellyfish does whatever a real jellyfish can do, and then some. A jellyfish's advantage is a long, fancy word for something that it does: chemoreception. That means that it can sense various chemicals in the water and guide itself toward them. Since jellborgs were invented to find and clean up ocean pollution, all you need to do is to leave a trail of pollution for them. Drop something in the ocean, and the jellborgs will find it. Then, they'll clean it up as they approach you. Not only that, but they can signal each other. One jellborg finds something, and it electronically announces it to any others in the area, wherever they are. The others usually join the party within a few minutes."

"Hold on a moment," said Leah. "You're suggesting that we drop your little robotic jellyfish into the Red Sea to attract Bobby the Brute's stolen jellyfish robots, and that way we'll find out where they came from and where he hid his little electronic controller, the 'fob' thingy, or whatever he called it."

"Exactly!" answered Dilip. "Then, you can just dive down, grab his little fob and use it to turn off his bombs."

"Unless Rahulla Allijabulla gets to it first," said Yaakov.

"Sounds risky," said Leah.

"Actually," replied Yehuda, "it sounds kind of fun!"

Aharon Sapir spoke up for the first time in a while. "You know something? It sounds like a worthwhile plan, and it doesn't involve any danger to you. The security over there at Timna Valley Park is already on the alert, and I'm sure they'd appreciate a little extra help. Besides, those jellyfish robots aren't actually harmful at all, are they? I can jet you over to Israel starting tomorrow afternoon. You'll land at Timna Airport, head over to the beach at Eilat, and get to work. I'll supply you with whatever you need – scuba gear, wetsuits, and anything else."

"Sir, the whole thing sounds kind of crazy to me," answered Leah, sharply. "I mean, none of us have ever been scuba diving in our lives. And, who says that those fake jellyfish are even there? Maybe Bobby the Brute made the whole thing up. "

"There's a first time for everything," replied the billionaire with a smile. "I can even get you scuba lessons. Hey, I've never flown down here in a big rush from Santa Barbara at night, either. But with a private jet, a lot of wacky possibilities seem less crazy."

"Can we go, Imma?" asked Yaakov, with excitement. "Please? I really want to learn scuba diving. And if we don't at least try, Rahulla might find that controller first, or Bobby's time bombs might just go off anyway. Come on! Please? It'll just be a few days. I won't be missing school!"

"The boy has a point, Leah," said Yehuda. "And it'll give the kids something to do."

She sat back in her chair and let out a breath. "Oh, all right."

7 YAAKOV'S DEEP DIVE

"Okay, Yaakov," called Gal Babash from the dock, in a powerful, thickly accented voice. "Come on! Time to jump in!"

Gal and his brother, Tal, two diving instructors, ran an undersea tour operation. They called it "Diving Deep with Gal and Tal," but Yaakov was not about to dive very deeply. Yosef was already underwater, moving himself around with a large fishing net in his hands.

Yaakov stood on a five-foot raft, staring through his mask at the calm blue surface of the Red Sea and feeling both excited and ridiculous. The scene around Yaakov looked like something out of a glossy brochure, and the Tuesday afternoon sunlight felt just a bit too bright for his tired eyes. It was hot today, but he told himself that at least he wasn't in the Mojave Desert or on Djerba. The raft floated close to Coral Beach, a quiet and lesser-known pocket of Israel's southern coast, near the city of Eilat. On his feet, Yaakov wore a couple of comfortable blue fins. He also wore a tightly fitting wetsuit, and the regulator in his mouth was attached to a hose that connected him to an air tank. Today, Yaakov was about to try a new and totally unfamiliar activity: snuba diving.

As the Peretz brothers had recently learned, snuba diving is a simpler version of scuba diving, invented mainly for beginners. Rather than carrying a heavy air tank on his or her back, a snuba diver connects to an air tank that sits on a raft. A hose connects the air tank to a regulator, a breathing device held in the diver's mouth. The hose connecting also helps guide the diver to whatever depth he or she wants. Most snuba dives are not deeper than about twenty feet.

Yaakov had never even heard the word "snuba" until the day before. And what a busy day had just passed! Aharon Sapir had arranged everything quickly, as the wealthy man generally seemed able to do, with no more than the push of a button or a couple of phone calls. The Peretzes rose early on Monday morning and hurriedly packed their bags for a noontime flight to Israel in Aharon's private jet, leaving from Burbank Airport. Aharon himself needed to fly to Israel anyway, to attend a winemaking convention in the Golan Heights, a mountain range near the country's northern border. His plane landed at Timna Airport, located at the southern end of Israel.

Their fifteen-hour flight and the ten-hour time difference between Israel and Los Angeles meant a full-day journey for the Peretz family. Shortly after landing, it was a quick hop over to a posh hotel in Eilat, where Yaakov's jet-lagged parents and little sister almost instantly collapsed into their beds. Meanwhile, Yaakov and Yosef hopped onto a bus and headed straight to the beach for their underwater experience. As promised, Aharon Sapir voluntarily paid the family's every expense, including today's dive.

Today was the day to foil Bobby the Brute yet again, and to put an end to Rahulla Allijabulla's criminal career. Their long flight over the Atlantic Ocean had given the Peretzes plenty of time to flesh out all of the details of their Grand Plan.

The dive was Part One. In his right hand, Yaakov held Dilip Sitoop's artificial jellyfish, a foot-long robot with tentacles that looked quite real. On landing in the water, this device was expected to begin sending out search signals, seeking any other such robots that may have been floating nearby. It was also supposed to lure those jellborgs out of hiding by leaking a trail of fake human blood (just reddish-purplish food coloring with an odor) into the sea. With this robot's help, the boys planned to draw Bobby the Brute's supposed hoard of stolen jellyfish robots out of hiding, leading the boys to the electronic controller that stored the passcode for the pirate's bombs. Jellborgs were built with chemoreception ability, as Dilip Sitoop had recently explained, and would "sniff out" the fake blood in the water; the jellborgs were going to head directly into the boys' net, which Yosef now carried. They were also expected to lead the boys to Bobby the Brute's little electronic controller, his "fob." After snatching Bobby the Brute's fob, the boys planned to replace it with the decoy that Yaakov now held in his left hand.

Remember the nose squeeze, Yaakov told himself, leaping off the raft and splashing into the Red Sea. As soon as he had plunged under the water, he took a quick glance to his right. Spotting Yosef, he flashed his brother the "thumbs-up" sign, which Yosef immediately returned.

Yaakov was then struck by the breathtaking scene before him. He felt as if he had been transported instantly to another world. The Red Sea was an underwater jungle, teeming with complex and beautiful aquatic creatures. Brightly colored tropical fish of numerous varieties swam past him. On the sea floor beneath him lay anemones, sea urchins, crabs, oysters, and many living things that he could not identify. Several blue spotted stingrays darted past him.

Of course, there was no way to ignore the coral. Hundreds of species of coral inhabit the Red Sea, and Yaakov felt excited to begin exploring the reef that lay beneath him. Swimming continuously, Yaakov navigated over the bumpy, spiky coral colonies that seemed to form brownish and greenish mountain ranges. Maneuvering through the amazingly clear water, Yaakov imagined that he was piloting a rescue helicopter over the Himalayas, searching for a stranded climber. He also felt a little bit guilty about polluting this sea with food coloring.

After several minutes, Yosef swam over to Yaakov, tapped him on the shoulder and pointed to a bunch of jellyfish that seemed to be moving toward the two boys. There were about a dozen of them, each no more than a foot long, with a mushroom-shaped head attached to a clump of stringy tentacles. Yaakov knew that these creatures generally moved by simply floating on sea currents rather than actively propelling themselves through the water; still, their slow but steady approach was discomforting. Were these squishy creatures real or robotic? He needed a closer look, but reminded himself that real jellyfish could sting.

Yaakov let go of his robot and used his right hand to signal Yosef to wait in his place. To his relief, the passing jellyfish seemed to move in a rag-tag line, as in a children's game of "Follow the Leader," rather than a swarm; that would make it easier to find their starting point. Because they purposely moved in a straight path, rather than just floating by, Yaakov suspected that he had just found Bobby's hoard of robot guards. He swam quickly toward the back of the line of sea creatures, searching for any clues to their nature and their starting point. Each of these floating blobs seemed quite realistic, as robotic jellyfish were designed to look. From a fairly short distance, it was hard to tell even Dilip Sitoop's model from the real thing; however, by looking closely, he could detect a few dimly glowing LED lights and switches coming from the middle of its bulbous head. The lights were meant to simulate a property of real jellyfish: bioluminescence, the ability of jellyfish and some other creatures to produce light from the insides of their bodies.

Yaakov squinted closely at the squishy things that paraded past him. He began to get a bit frantic, and then remembered that, when snuba diving, slow and relaxed breathing was best. Nothing really appeared unusual about any of these jellyfish, until Yaakov noticed the tiny letters imprinted on the last one in the line. Careful not to touch it, he squinted at its thickest tentacle and clearly read the words "MADE IN SINGAPORE." Staring intently at the object's head, Yaakov began to notice the tiny gears and gyros that propelled the little invertebrate through the water. These things were robotic indeed! Attracted by the reddish dye coming from Dilip Sitoop's robot, they had swum some distance toward the boys.

But where had they started? Yaakov scanned the sea floor for any clues to the spot where this jellborg parade had started. Scanning the rough, spiky and tubular formations beneath him, he began to doubt whether anything really could remain buried in this coral. A scary thought briefly entered his mind: perhaps Bobby the Brute's little controller had simply floated away, and now drifted uselessly in the ocean, leaving no chance to disable the explosives hidden in Timna Park. He pushed away that thought and began examining a dim glow that came from a crevice within a purplish coral colony just a few feet away. The entire colony seemed to vibrate in a bizarre manner. There was no way to check out the glow from that crevice without diving deeper.

It was only then that Yaakov began to notice the dull but persistent aches in both his ears. Earaches were the hardest thing about air travel and swimming, and he had just done both of those activities within the past day. Yaakov had never swum to the very bottom of a swimming pool; the pain in his ears simply made it impossible whenever he tried. And he truly hated landing in airplanes. On some flights, he had simply wished he could snap his fingers and be transported magically to Baggage Claim, instead of having to suffer the agony of increasing air pressure and the intense pain that it caused. Somehow, he had already recovered from his most recent flight, only to be torturing his ears again with a dive.

Do the nose trick, he reminded himself. He was afraid to try the nose trick, though. What if the trick didn't work? It was too hard to imagine what might happen if he couldn't release that pressure from his ears and simply shot down to that glowing crevice anyway. He knew that he had to conquer his fear. Just a few days earlier, he had pushed past his fear of heights to escape from the *Pacific Dreamer*, and had bossed around a dangerous criminal by using a fishing pole to make himself seem tough and threatening; now was not the time to let some pressure on his ears stop him from doing what he had to do.

With his free hand, Yaakov squeezed his nostrils together and blew through them as hard as he could. In an instant, the awful pressure on his ears was gone. He felt like a free person once again, able to go wherever he pleased. Staring at the glowing hole in the coral beneath him, Yaakov pushed straight downward for a closer look.

From this new depth, he clearly saw yet another jellborg. This one had somehow gotten stuck on its way out of the crevice, and was positioned oddly. Its little mechanical gears kept working, causing it to press repeatedly against the walls of the coral colony that contained it, and forcing the entire structure to vibrate unnaturally. Yaakov stuck his head several inches away from the hole and peered directly inside it. He couldn't believe his eyes! There, inside the coral, lay a sealed plastic sandwich bag containing a tiny electronic gadget. The stuck jellborg illuminated the little device, and Yaakov probably would have missed it if not for the light that the jellborg provided. The gadget was small enough to fit into Yaakov's hand, probably about the size of a keychain. It seemed rather simple, with no buttons or switches of any kind. There was a little display screen on it, but Yaakov couldn't read it in the dim light. Was that little gadget Bobby the Brute's passcode controller, which the pirate had called a "fob?"

Yaakov looked upwards and motioned for Yosef to come closer. By now, Yosef had caught a bunch of floating jellborgs in his fishing net, which he now held in both hands. When Yosef approached him, Yaakov pointed to the little robot that was now trapped in the coral. Yosef looked at Yaakov and gave him a nod. Then, he moved a few feet away from Yaakov and prepared to catch his next prey. Yaakov extended his right leg and began to nudge the trapped robot with his diving fin. In about ten seconds, he managed to free it. It floated upward, and Yosef caught it easily in his net. Right away, Yaakov swooped down toward the hole, stuck his hand inside it, and grabbed the plastic baggie. He then tossed his little black decoy into the hole. After doing so, he gave Yosef a look of victory, holding the pirate's gadget in his left hand and giving him another "thumbs up" sign with his right.

The two boys looked upward and began ascending, carrying their discoveries back to the shore. As he swam, Yaakov gripped the plastic baggie with all of the strength that his left hand could muster. His jetlag now began to catch up with him, and he knew that he needed a lot of sleep. Still, all that he wanted to do was to run straight to Timna Valley Park and shut down Bobby the Brute's explosives. It would have to wait, though. He knew that he wouldn't be able to manage Part Two of the Grand Plan by himself.

He was about halfway back to the surface when he felt the sting. A sudden, sharp pain pierced the calf of his left leg. It was followed by a powerful burn that grew more intense by the second. Some creature or object had just stabbed him, and Yaakov wanted to scream. But screaming was impossible underwater, and swimming was getting harder with every passing second. Soon, the burning became a throbbing pain that shot up through his knee and thigh. *I can't drown*, thought Yaakov. *I'm too young for that.* He knew that he had to make it out of the water while he could still move his leg, because the air tank attached to his regulator would not last forever.

The next few moments felt like an eternity. Moving both arms and his right leg in faster and more frantic strokes, he continued to propel himself upward, closer and closer to the blurry, dark shadow that hovered above him. The raft! Reaching it now meant life itself. As he swam, he tightened his grip on the plastic baggie and repeated the same four-word sentence in his mind: *Don't drop the bag.*

Finally, he reached the surface. He stuck his head out of the water and grabbed onto the little raft for dear life. Yosef was already sitting on it, holding his regulator in one hand and a fishing net full of small jellborgs in the other.

"What took you so long?" he asked. "And what's wrong?" he then added, with a worried expression, obviously reading the look of pain on Yaakov's face.

Yaakov pulled his regulator out of his mouth and dropped it onto the raft, along with the plastic bag. "Help me on!" he shouted. "Something bit my leg! It hurts!"

Pulling his brother by the arms, Yosef helped Yaakov climb aboard the raft. They both sat there and examined Yaakov's injury. The gaping red gash in his skin was marked with purplish tracks, and was surrounded by many tiny needles. On looking at his wound, Yaakov began to feel his strength leaving him. He dreaded that he might soon vomit.

Yosef looked toward the dock and began waving his arms and calling the diving instructors. "Gal! Tal! Come quick! Yaakov's been hurt!"

Instantly, both instructors dove into the water and darted toward the raft. They reached the two brothers in a moment, and quickly concluded that Yaakov had been stung by a real jellyfish, or a "medusa," as it was called in Hebrew.

"No problem," Gal reassured Yaakov, as Tal jumped back into the water to get his first aid kit. "You'll be all better, *chick chock*," he added, using the common Hebrew slang for "right away."

Tal treated the wound with vinegar, removed all of the stingers, and applied a cold pack while Gal pulled the raft back to the dock. Several minutes later, Tal applied a bandage and an antibiotic ointment to Yaakov's wound, while the two boys sat on the shore, atop beach towels. Tal also gave Yaakov an extra package of bandages and a few tubes of the ointment. Afterwards, Gal and Tal left. The two boys thanked them as the diving instructors as they departed, and then lay back on the sand to rest in the warm afternoon sun.

"Well, forget about going to Timna Park tomorrow," said Yosef. "You can barely even walk."

"No way," answered Yaakov, forcefully. "We're going. Jellyfish won't stop us."

8 THE HUNT

Rachel burst into hysterical laughter as soon as the statues came into view. Three giant figurines, built to resemble ancient Egyptians, stood on the left side of the Copper Road, the path leading into Timna Valley Park, and greeted the Peretzes as their rented driverless vehicle transported them towards the park entrance. It was Wednesday morning, and the family planned on spending the next couple of days at the park. They were now only about 17 miles north of Eilat, where Yaakov and his brother had swum under a clear and vibrant sea just a day earlier.

The contrast between yesterday's Red Sea diving expedition and this morning's jaunt to the desert couldn't be starker. Now that Bobby the Brute's keychain-sized electronic controller, his so-called "fob," was in the Peretz family's possession, it was time to carry out Part Two of their Grand Plan. The detonator that this fob controlled was hidden somewhere within the enormous Timna Valley. The plan was to camp near the manmade Timna Lake, explore the area, and search for a way to thwart Rahulla Allijabulla from raiding King Solomon's mines.

The statue closest to the Copper Road looked like a Pharaoh, wearing a long desert robe and a headdress. To its left stood statues of a man wearing a white cloth, with a staff in his hand, and a lady in a long gown, holding a basket.

"Look at that guy!" exclaimed Rachel from the backseat, pointing to the Pharaoh. "He looks like Chief Sitting Bull."

Yosef rolled his eyes. "Please! Would you settle down, Rachel?"

Rachel ignored the rebuke and continued laughing. "Look at his hat!" Then, she went back to reading her book, a classic children's novel entitled *Junie B. Jones Has a Monster Under Her Bed.*

"It's not even 9:00 in the morning!" continued Yosef. "Imma, if I knew we were going to Legoland, I would have just stayed in the hotel."

"Just try to enjoy it, Yosef," Leah answered from the front passenger seat. She turned around and faced him. "Remember what we talked about last night. Make it positive."

"Okay, okay," he responded in a low voice.

"Can everyone please be quiet?" asked Yaakov, sitting between his siblings. "I'm trying to listen."

An audio program streamed into the vehicle through its speaker system, describing the beauty and history of Timna Park. In clear, barely accented English, a woman named Dr. Orit Levi-Iparon told her listeners about the natural sandstone formations carved by the desert and wind over the ages. She encouraged visitors to visit the various sights, including the Temple of Hathor, built by the ancient Egyptians to worship a pagan deity, and to admire the rock carvings that displayed various objects and scenes, like Egyptian battle gear and hunters chasing their prey. Some of those prey, said Dr. Levi-Iparon, included the ibexes that still roamed the park, alongside gazelles. Yaakov found most of this information pretty interesting, and paid close attention while his siblings busied themselves with their toys or read. He was particularly interested in the narrator's description of the copper mines. In addition to King Solomon's mines, located at Slaves' Hill, the park was said to contain many ancient mine shafts. As he listened, he struggled to think of any clues that might lead him to the explosive devices that Bobby the Brute had bragged about hiding somewhere inside the park.

Dr. Levi-Iparon concluded her speech with advertisements for the family recreation that the park had to offer, including a multimedia presentation on copper mining and "the many fascinating uses of this important element." Yaakov ignored the rest of the recording.

They parked at the entrance and unloaded their supplies, including bottled water, sunscreen, and snacks. On stepping out of the car, Yaakov loaded his backpack onto both shoulders. In addition to food and water, his backpack contained the jellborgs that he and Yosef had found in the Red Sea, a closed plastic food storage container holding their leftover supply of artificial blood, a flashlight, and Bobby the Brute's fob. Of course, he had also packed plenty of extra bandages and antibiotic ointment for the continued treatments that his recently injured leg still required. From where he stood, Yaakov could see distant mountains and sandstone formations. The task ahead of him seemed overwhelming. Where, among those many geologic formations that filled the vast valley ahead of him, could that detonator possibly be hidden?

Yehuda led the way into the park, beginning with a brief stop at the visitor center. There, the Peretzes picked up four maps of the area. To make things easier for tourists, many parks and other recreational facilities printed their maps onto thin sheets equipped with throwaway flexible electronic circuits. Each map was basically a display screen showing a diagram of all of the park's attractions and a blinking red arrow that moved as the map was carried. The printed words "You are here" accompanied the arrow and traveled across the screen with it.

In addition to securing the maps, Yehuda purchased cheap cell phones for the boys, Leah and himself. Next, he asked the park staff a few questions about the overnight camping facilities.

Soon, it was time to part ways. The Peretzes left the building, and then huddled around Yehuda and his map to plan their search for the hidden detonator.

"I think it'll be best for us split up into separate groups for while," Yehuda told the others. "That way, we can spread out through the park and take different sections at once. We need to focus on the major touristy areas, where there are likely to be crowds. Bobby the Brute probably wanted to set up a major scare, and create a lot of chaos, so that he wouldn't be noticed slipping in to steal from the big dig at Slaves' Hill. We can all meet back at one common area around lunchtime. What does everyone think of that?"

"Wait," said Rachel. "Are we just gonna go around looking for a little machine the whole time? That's boring!"

"Rachel, I'll tell you what," said Leah. "I'll take you to the play area at the lake."

"What lake?" asked Rachel, excitedly.

"It's called Timna Lake, dear." Leah pointed to a picture of the lake on Yehuda's map. "You see? There are paddle boats there, and you can play in the sand and with copper coins. We can both have fun there, and you can spend some time helping me look around for that device. You can help me set up our tents, too. Does that sound okay?"

"I guess so," said Rachel, with a slightly suspicious expression. "But why do we have to do that anyway, Imma? Didn't you tell us the security guards were already trying to stop the bombs?"

"Yes, Rachel," her mother answered, "but we want to help them in any way we can."

Yehuda pointed at some regions on his map opposite the lake. "I'll start poking around at Slaves' Hill itself. They're supposed to start the dig there tomorrow, so it's the most obvious place to search. Then, I'll go and check out these other spots that look like tourist attractions: the Sphinx and the Temple of Hathor. Why don't Yaakov and Yosef check out the other side of the park?"

"Why?" asked Yosef with a wry smile. "Too many hiking trails for the old fogeys?"

Yehuda gave him a look. "That's *mature* fogeys to you, my son. Yeah, you kids are still young and flexible enough to handle all those caves and things." He pointed to several places on the map as he continued talking. "You see, guys? You can check out the ancient mines, the arches, the Roman cave, and all those spots. You can still handle all those things."

"You're not that old, Abba," Yaakov chimed in, hoping to encourage his father.

"Thanks, Yaakov," Yehuda answered.

Yaakov felt a sinking sensation. He suspected that their entire search was doomed to be a waste of time. Something didn't quite feel right about searching the park's obvious tourist attractions.

"Abba, can we rent bikes?" asked Yosef. He pointed to some stick-figure diagrams of cyclists on the map, and moved his finger along the adjacent dotted lines that indicated bicycle paths.

"I don't see why not," answered Yehuda. "Mr. Sapir's paying for the whole thing, and he said we could spend on whatever we needed."

"It's an excellent idea," agreed Leah. "You'll cover a lot more ground that way, and faster. Of course, if you're looking for a small object, it may be anywhere. Remember to get helmets, too. You need them."

"All right," said Yehuda. "Then it's settled. We'll do the best we can, and then we'll meet back at the restaurant for lunch."

"Yes," replied Leah, "and while we eat, we can talk about whatever we've seen so far. Ready for some fun, Rachel?"

"Yeah," said Rachel, "but I don't want to go on the paddle boats by myself."

"Of course I'll come with you, sweetie," answered Leah, cheerily. She took Rachel by the hand and began to lead her in the direction of Timna Lake. "Let's go." After walking with Rachel for a moment, she turned her head and called back to her family, "It gets very hot here in the middle of the day, so don't forget to wear sunscreen, everyone! And drink plenty of water. Oh, and boys, remember your bike helmets!"

Yaakov and Yosef picked out mountain bikes and headgear from Ofer's Cycle Shop by the park entrance. Their father quickly helped them take care of the transaction, and the boys were off.

It only took a few minutes of cycling for Yaakov to realize just how vast this park was. From the entrance, the two boys followed a trail that headed northward through the region known as the Sasgon Valley. Soon, Mount Michrot came into view. The boys continued in their original basic direction, navigating over rocky and hilly terrain, and eventually passed the mountain.

Their cycling tour was certainly nothing like the many cushy Sunday afternoon bike rides that the Peretz kids had taken through parks in L.A. and Beverly Hills, on painted, smoothly paved paths. This ride was very demanding, though far more exciting than any that Yaakov had ever taken. At times, he found himself having to squint at the ground and guess where the trail continued. The boys remained together, usually with Yaakov leading the way; however, in some places, the trail widened enough to allow them to ride side by side.

As the morning progressed, the air became gradually warmer, and Yaakov wondered how much sweat one boy's body could possibly contain. Still, he pressed onward. For a brief moment, he thought that it would have been smarter not to ride with such a heavy pack on his back. Then, he told himself that it probably didn't make a difference. His knee and thigh muscles grew so sore that he soon forgot about his jellyfish sting.

Throughout the journey, Yaakov kept his eyes out for any suspicious objects that may have been left around him. He saw nothing but brownish rock and sandstone. At times, he even felt silly for coming to such a majestic region to search for a small detonator.

After a time, Yaakov and Yosef reached an intersection. They stopped their bikes, gulped down some water and consulted their maps. As the electronic blinking arrow informed them, their bike path veered sharply to the right, continuing in a loop that led almost back to the park entrance. To their left, it became a hiking trail, and not a simple one. The trail led upwards and into the steep Timna Cliffs. Panting and out of breath, Yaakov placed his right hand on his forehead to block the sunlight from entering his eyes and took a look at the steep and jagged terrain before him. *Could that weasely pirate named Robert have planted explosives up in those cliffs?* he wondered. *What would he have accomplished, besides starting an avalanche of boulders?*

"I don't think we're gonna find anything up there, Yosef," said Yaakov.

"Yeah," Yosef agreed, "let's turn right and head back to the entrance."

"Sure." said Yaakov, "We can return the bikes pretty soon and then get on one of those easier trails, like the one leading up to the Chariots. We probably have a better chance of finding something over there. Besides, I'll need a break by then."

"Me too." Yosef steered his bike to his right and started pedaling. "I'll lead the way this time!" he called as he started down the trail.

Yaakov quickly caught up to his younger brother.

The cycling path led the boys to the east for a fair distance. Before long, they made another right turn and headed southward. They continued on this stretch until finding themselves back at the paved road that led into the park.

As soon as they reached the road, Yaakov stopped his bike and climbed off of it. Yosef climbed off his bike, as well.

"My leg is killing is me," said Yaakov. "I need to sit down for a while."

The brothers sat in the dirt by the side of the road and drank more water. Afterwards, Yaakov took off his helmet and backpack. Then he checked his left leg. Some of the scabs that had formed over his wound had come open, and the leg was now bleeding again. He removed some more bandage material and a bottle of ointment from his backpack. Next, he took off the old bandages, and poured a bit of water from his bottle onto the wound. He then dried the area with a small paper towel, applied some ointment to his new bandage, and used it cover the wound again.

Meanwhile, Yosef stared intently at his map. When Yaakov was finished dressing his wound, Yosef pointed to some lines. "Look," he said, "we can stay on the road until we get to this short hiking trail near Spiral Hill. It's the fastest way to get up to the Chariots." When he mentioned the Chariots, he tapped a little blue dot on the map.

Instantly, a recorded voice began to speak. "The Chariots," it announced, in a dull tone. "Ages ago, Egyptian miners engraved the stones where they worked with fascinating art. Near these mining tunnels and pits, you will find pictures of animals like ostriches and ibexes, as well as the men who hunted them, all carved into the ancient stones. Drawings of chariots are clearly visible as well. Step up into the cave entrance, where…"

Yosef tapped the blue light again, and the voice stopped. "Okay, that's boring enough for me. Let's just go there and take a look around."

"All right," replied Yaakov. "Give me a minute."

Holding onto his mountain bike, he slowly pulled himself up to a standing position. The boys then walked their bicycles back to the park entrance and returned them. As soon as they did so, Yaakov's left leg began to ache again, so the boys proceeded rather slowly. After what felt like forever, they reached the beginning of the trail leading to the Chariots.

Yaakov took one look at the trail, and his heart sank. "It's uphill, isn't it?"

"Just at the end," answered Yosef.

Suddenly, Yaakov's phone rang. He pulled it out of his pocket and answered it. "Hello?"

"Hi, dear," greeted Leah.

"Hi, Imma."

"Are you boys having a good time?" asked Leah.

"Yeah," replied Yaakov, "but this place is big. And it's taking us a really long time to get around."

"I understand," answered his mother. "Have you found anything yet?"

"No," said Yaakov, "there's just way too much here. Those bombs can be anywhere! So can the detonator! And there are so many holes, and caves, and tunnels. How are we supposed to figure out where Bobby the Brute wanted to strike? We have to know what in the world he was thinking when he set up his bombs.

Where would he actually want his explosions to go off? That's what we still don't know. Did Abba find anything at King Solomon's Mines?"

"Nope," replied Leah. "In fact, it's been closed for two weeks, while they get ready for their big dig. There are big green fences around the whole area. They yelled at him when he tried to get in. Look, Yaakov, it's a little after 11:30. Why don't you boys make your way over to the restaurant near the lake? Do you see it on your maps? It's called 'King Solomon's Inn.' You can rest up there, and we'll have some lunch."

"Okay, Imma. Bye." He hung up. "Yosef, Imma wants us to turn around meet her at the restaurant near the lake with Abba and Rachel."

Yosef shrugged. "Why not? I'm getting hungry anyway."

It was quite a walk to the restaurant. The boys decided to stay on the paved road rather than stress Yaakov's leg on the hiking trails, even though those trails seemed to lead to the same destination more quickly. After about five minutes of walking, Yaakov noticed a small crowd of about two dozen tourists gathered ahead of him, all standing around and listening to their tour guide. A quick glance at his map showed that they were visiting the Temple of Hathor, the old Egyptian temple that had been discovered in the center of Timna Valley many years earlier. He suddenly had an idea.

"You know what?" he asked his brother.

"What?"

Yaakov stopped walking and pointed in the direction of the temple and the nearby crowd. "Let's see what's over there, Yosef. I think Bobby could have easily hidden something in a place like that."

"A place like what?" asked Yosef.

"That old Egyptian temple," answered Yaakov. "Why not? There are probably still a lot of little artifacts and things buried there. And it doesn't look guarded or anything. It would have been no problem for him to just bury a little detonator in there and walk away."

Yosef looked at Yaakov as if he had just announced that he was really an alien from the planet Rahelio Zambista. "I think you got a little too much sun today."

"You don't believe me?" asked Yaakov.

"Yaakov, come on," replied Yosef, sounding annoyed. "First of all, a lot of people walk past that thing every day. Don't you think somebody would have noticed a little gizmo made out of a car door opener in there by now? And second, what do you want to do, jump into the exhibit when nobody's looking and just start trying to dig it up?"

"Okay, okay," said Yaakov, "don't get upset. I just think it's worth taking a little look. Anyway, it's sort of on the way to the restaurant, right?"

Yosef rolled his eyes and sighed. "Quickly. And I'm not sticking around to make a whole stop out of it. I barely ate anything today."

The boys turned from the paved road and headed down a relatively tame hiking trail towards the Temple of Hathor. They arrived in front of the site just in time to hear the tour guide, a middle-aged, slightly bald man wearing casual clothes and light brown sunglasses, describe the things that had been discovered at that spot over the past several decades. Yaakov and Yosef stood in the back of the crowd, next to a large man and woman who both wore white T-shirts bearing the words "I Left My Heart in Texas."

"You see," announced the guide, with a mild Israeli accent, "what people leave behind can be very important for future generations who want to understand their past. Many, many treasures have been unearthed from this site, thousands of artifacts. They are valuable to us, because they tell us about the very advanced people who used to inhabit the area. For example, we have found the royal seals of most of the Pharaohs who ruled in a two-hundred-year period. We have found objects made of copper, little leopard statues, beads, and sculptures of the Egyptian idol. Also, we know that in a later period, the Midianites came to this area. Here at the temple, they left behind pottery and metal jewelry, including a very interesting copper snake."

As the tour guide spoke, Yaakov quietly took off his backpack, opened it, and removed the plastic bag that he had found in the Red Sea. *Those aren't the only treasures around here*, he thought. He removed the fob from the baggie and began waving it around, while struggling to see what was in the Temple of Hathor.

"What in the world are you doing?" whispered Yosef.

"I'm trying to see where something of this size, or maybe a little bigger, would fit in there without being noticed."

"Can't you do that later?" Yosef whispered back, harshly. "*We're gonna be noticed if you don't stop that!*"

The man in the white T-shirt turned and looked at both boys. "Hey, quiet, kids," he snapped, in a sharp

Texas twang. "I'm trying to hear this."

"Sorry," said Yaakov, meekly.

"Let's get out of here," whispered Yosef.

With his mind still on the archaeological site that he and his brother had just seen, Yaakov turned around and headed back onto the hiking trail. As he did so, he casually slung his backpack over his shoulders again, without paying much attention to his surroundings. He couldn't stop thinking about that sunken building filled with buried artifacts. The boys stayed on the hiking trail until it became a bike path, and then followed that path all the way to Timna Lake.

Their father greeted them in front of King Solomon's Inn, with a wide smile and his open hands outstretched. Whenever he met his kids, Yehuda seemed genuinely happy to see them. "Boys, welcome! How are you?"

"Hi, Abba!" answered Yosef. "How am I? Hungry."

Yaakov looked up at his father, briefly. "Hello, Abba," he said.

"Hello, Yaakov. Come, guys, we found a nice, cool place to sit inside. It's way too hot out here. We've got some pita bread with hummus waiting for you. And there's falafel, and some dips, and all that. We even managed to find – or dig up, heh-heh – some pizza!" He was always coming up with doubtfully funny puns, and telling jokes like, "You know what's the difference between a guitar and a fish? You can tune a guitar…but you can't *tuna fish!*"

The three of them soon joined Leah and Rachel at a wide table inside the somewhat crowded building. Rachel was the first one to greet the boys, holding up a slice of cheese pizza as she did.

"Hi, guys!" called Rachel. "Guess what? We got

pizza. See? It's right there: the regular kind and some with yucky toppings on them."

"Hmm," answered Yaakov, sitting on a chair next to Rachel, "I might like some of those yucky toppings."

"Like what," asked Rachel, "mushrooms? Ew! Those things are gross."

Those words hit Yaakov like a ton of bricks. He sat up straight in his chair. "That's it!" he exclaimed.

"Lower your voice, please," said Leah. "There are people here."

"Imma, I just figured it out!" continued Yaakov, speaking quickly but trying to sound quiet. "The Mushroom! That has to be the place where Bobby the Brute hid his bombs. And the detonator can't be too far off, because he made it from a remote-control car opener."

The Mushroom was an enormous sandstone formation in Timna Valley, a stone that had been formed by the wind into the shape of a giant mushroom. It was clearly visible on the Peretzes' maps. In fact, Timna included two such structures. One was simply called "The Mushroom," because it resembled one. The other was located next to a much shorter rock formation; that pair of stones was known as "The Mushroom and a Half."

"Why are you so sure?" asked Yehuda, who now sat on the seat across from Yaakov, finishing a piece of pita bread.

"Don't you remember what Bobby said to Rahulla on Anacapa Island? Rahulla told him that Bobby would rather be out of prison, because the food was better, and Bobby made a remark about the awful mushroom soup that they used to make him eat there. He said he'd never forgive them for doing that to him. So, if he was out to do some damage here anyway, what better place would there be for him to attack? It would be kind of like a poetic…what do they call that, Imma?"

"You mean poetic justice?" she asked, while filling a pocket of pita bread with falafel balls and finely diced chunks of tomatoes and cucumbers.

"Yeah, poetic justice, in his sick mind. It'd be Bobby's perfect chance to get his revenge on the prison *and* steal some treasures at the same time."

Yosef gave him a look. "Treasures?"

"Yes, treasures," answered Yaakov, matter-of-factly. "You heard what that tour guide said."

"Do you always have to remember everything?" asked Yosef.

Yaakov ignored the insolent question and faced his parents. "Well, I want to go over to the Mushroom and see if we can find that detonator there. Can I just go and check it out right now?"

"Not until I've taken another look at your leg, Yaakov," answered Leah.

"And you've eaten something," added Yehuda.

"And you're not going alone," said Leah. "Yosef has to go with you."

Yosef sat in his chair, munching on a falafel sandwich. "We were almost over there just a little while ago," he responded, with a mouth full of food. He chewed a bit more, swallowed, and continued: "I guess I'll come along. There's not much else to do around here."

After lunch and the traditional Grace After Meals, the family took a brief stroll to their campsite by Lake Timna. As they walked, Rachel informed Yosef that,

105

actually, there was quite a lot to do around there. She had already filled bottles with sand, minted copper coins, pedaled their way around the lake in a boat, and seen a model of the Jewish Tabernacle, the ancient, portable Temple structure that existed prior to the construction of the stone Temple in Jerusalem.

The family soon reached the rented tents that Leah had chosen that morning. Yaakov lay on a mat inside one of them while his mother examined his bandages, washed the area around his wound with water, and redressed his wound. As she did so, he toyed with the zippers on his backpack.

"Remember that you're supposed to change these three times a day," she told him calmly, when she was finished.

"I know," answered Yaakov, "and I already did that once this morning."

"Good," she replied. "Does it still hurt?"

"Not really."

"Okay," said Leah, "but rest for a while before you take any hikes."

"I will."

Yaakov noticed a slight bulge in one of his backpack's outer pockets. He didn't remember placing anything in it recently, so he zipped open the pocket and stuck his hand inside it. As his hands felt the object that it contained, he remembered an incident that had occurred back in California several weeks earlier. This object was his BotConv, a small device that allowed people to tell, or even to whisper, voice commands to their robots. It had come in quite handy on Aharon Sapir's lawn in Santa Barbara, when Yaakov and family had found themselves surrounded by old-fashioned pirates while their navigation robot sat in the family vehicle. A briefly whispered command to that robot had given the Peretzes the precious few seconds that they had needed to escape from a dangerous situation. Today, he had none of his trusted robots to come to his aid. He dropped the gadget back into his backpack and zipped it shut.

Later that afternoon, Yaakov and Yosef followed a long and winding path that led to the impressive formations known as the Mushroom and a Half. These two reddish stones stood out from the rest of the surrounding desert scene. The larger stone, known as the Mushroom, seemed to be about thirty feet tall and wider than any tree trunk that Yaakov had ever seen. Besides the many grooves and pockmarks all around it, the stone basically did resemble a mushroom. About twenty feet from this stone was the much shorter formation commonly known as the "Half" (even though it was less than half as tall as the Mushroom).

Their trail led right past the Half, and this stone formation was the one that the boys reached first. As they approached the Half, Yaakov noticed a tall man in a khaki outfit, who stood behind the Mushroom and fidgeted with something that seemed stuck inside a groove in the stone itself. Attached to his belt, he wore a holster that held a small handgun.

The man appeared very frustrated. In his left hand, he held a little black object. He kept looking from the object in his hand to the Mushroom, poking at something in the stone with the fingers of his right hand, looking back at the object that he held, and then muttering an upset expression.

Yaakov froze when he saw the man. He recognized

that sour-looking face. Then, he quickly looked at Yosef.

"That's him!" he whispered. "Quick, let's hide."

Yosef followed Yaakov behind to a spot behind the Half, where Yaakov figured that they couldn't be seen. Slowly, they moved their heads ever so slightly from behind the stone and took another look at the annoyed man.

"Yeah, that's him, all right," whispered Yosef. "It's Rahulla Allijabulla, dressed up as a park ranger. And he's got our decoy."

The decoy was a small piece of plastic, about the size of a car door opener, with a little digital display screen that showed seven numbers in a row. The numbers never changed, and there were no buttons or controls on it. Dilip Sitoop had quickly thrown together the device on Sunday night after leaving Babylon Grill, and had dropped it off at the Peretz home early on Monday morning. It was meant to fool Rahulla Allijabulla into thinking that he had found the passcode for Bobby the Brute's detonator, and now it seemed to be doing its job.

"Watch, Yosef," whispered Yaakov. "Here's the part where he gives up, throws the decoy on the ground, and leaves. Then, we move in."

As Yaakov had predicted, Rahulla soon muttered something like, "Stupid pirate!" Then, he threw the useless device onto the ground and stormed off, heading across the desert sand toward the other Mushroom, the lone rock formation that stood without a "Half" partner. When he was gone, the boys emerged from their hiding place.

Yaakov began to run toward the nearby Mushroom

stone, and immediately tripped over a rock.

"Ow!" he exclaimed, as he hit the ground, landing directly on his injured leg.

"Are you all right?" asked Yosef, standing near him.

"Yeah, I'm fine," he answered, with a pained expression. "Just go and take a look at the detonator."

Yosef approached the Mushroom, took a quick look into one of its crevices, and returned to Yaakov a moment later. "Yeah, it's there. It's jammed in very, very tightly. Just give me the real controller, and I'll go type in the code."

"Okay, one minute," answered Yaakov. He removed his backpack, opened its main pocket, and began to rummage through it. Inside, he found many things that he had expected to find: jellborgs, his container of fake blood, snack foods, bottled water, a flashlight, bandages, paper towels, ointment...and nothing else. "Uh oh."

Yosef gave him a troubled look. "What do you mean, 'uh-oh?'"

"Um, I can't exactly find it," answered Yaakov.

"What do you mean?"

Yaakov answered him without looking up. "I mean I lost it. It's gone."

Yosef bowed his head for a moment, groaned, and then looked at his brother. "We came all the way over here for nothing? That really sucks. Well, now what do we do?"

"I guess we'll have to think of a Plan B."

"Come on," said Yosef. "Let's head back to the campsite."

He helped Yaakov stand up, and the two boys hiked back down the trail together.

9 SNEAKING AROUND

"What do you want?" asked the gruff park ranger behind the simple brown desk. She was a stout, curly-haired, middle-aged woman in a khaki uniform that bore a nametag with the name "Anat" printed in Hebrew. The Peretzes stood opposite her in the ranger station.

Leah and Yehuda briefly told Anat their story, while the kids stood by, watching and listening. The parents took turns supplying Anat with the details of how they had uncovered Bobby the Brute's scheme and Rahulla Allijabulla's plan to set off an explosion in the park. They told Anat that their sons had even seen Rahulla attempting to activate Bobby's detonator, failing, and leaving in frustration. Leah made sure to describe her sons' dive in the Red Sea and their discovery of the pirate's jellborgs and passcode controller. As they spoke, Anat simply listened to their story with a stone-faced expression.

"Yes," she remarked, finally, in a cold tone. "We

know this already, about bombs. We have more security now, all over, checking the park. The whole park was even closed down on Monday, to check it out. Nobody found anything, the whole day. So don't 'fraid."

"But, now we know where the detonator is, and we have to do something about it," replied Yehuda. "We're asking you for help. Go to the Mushroom and a Half and check it out. See it all for yourself."

"Look," said Anat, leaning forward in her chair, "this is a big park. You overheard some people saying they wanted to set off a bomb somewhere inside. We have many people already checking it out. You saw the ranger checking. Okay, good!" Then, she leaned back again and lightened up a bit. "So, go and have a nice day at Timna Park. They will find everything. Don't 'fraid!"

"Me and my brother saw Rahulla Allijabulla messing with the detonator!" shouted Yaakov, speaking quickly. "It was stuck inside a crack in the Mushroom – you know, the big rock that's called the 'Mushroom,' near the one that's called the 'Half.' My brother even took a picture of it. Show him, Yosef."

Yosef held up his phone for Anat to see, and showed her a photo of the detonator wedged tightly into a crack in the Mushroom. He had taken the picture right after Yaakov's stumble earlier that afternoon. Anat glanced at the picture, and then dismissed it with the wave of a hand.

"Look," she told Yaakov, "don't be worrying with this. We have many park rangers here. They are checking everything. You saw one of them looking at the Mushroom? Okay, so everything will be fine."

Yaakov wasn't ready to give up so easily. "Well,

there's more to do. The actual *bombs* have to be found. We saw a guy trying to punch in our fake passcode. Then he threw our fake controller on the ground and left. All we have to do is put in the real passcode, from the real controller. Then we can turn off that detonator and stop the time bombs from going off. And, by the way, that man wasn't even a real park ranger. He was Rahulla Allijabulla."

Anat answered Yaakov abruptly. "Don't you tell me what is my job! The ranger looked like someone you know? Very nice. There are many people in the world. Some of them look alike. Once I even thought my grandfather looked like my uncle. We get tourists here from everywhere, all around the world."

"Help us, please," replied Yaakov, trying to sound polite but firm. He had come so far in his quest to foil Rahulla Allijabulla, and he was not about to quit now. "If you can go and search the area around the Mushroom, and by the Mushroom and a Half, and just find the actual bombs, you can get a bomb squad to deactivate them right away. Then, the detonator won't matter."

Anat rudely waved her hand again. "Just go and have a nice time. You have security. They are doing everything to help. Now go out of the office and do something else."

"Looks like we're back to Square One," Yehuda muttered, as they walked outside. Then he turned to Yaakov, with his typical smile and positive demeanor. "Don't worry, son, we'll think of something."

They headed back to the campsite, all agreeing to take the same paved bike path that Yaakov and Yosef had traveled earlier that day, a path that passed the

Temple of Hathor and led to the familiar area near Lake Timna. Leah instructed the others to keep their eyes open, and to keep checking the paved bike path and surroundings for the lost controller.

At one point, both of Yaakov's parents began asking him whether he had ever actually looked at the lost device and memorized its passcode. Yaakov explained patiently to them that, even if he had done so, it wouldn't have mattered, because the controller displayed the same seven-digit code for only five seconds at a time; after five seconds, that code disappeared, and a completely different code appeared on the little screen. Once the controller was lost, its codes were gone, too. Each code was totally random and lasted only five seconds, and there was no way to predict what the next code would be.

After a short while, Yaakov found himself lounging on a mat covered by a sleeping bag. At his mother's insistence, he rested his leg while the others continued searching for the lost controller. Leah wanted to retrace every step that the boys had possibly taken; perhaps they had overlooked some spot on their way back from the Temple of Hathor.

The tent was a boring place to be. Yaakov soon grew tired of staring at the same simple canvas walls, reviewing earlier steps over and over again in his mind. To relieve his boredom, he opened his backpack, pulled out the jellborgs, and started to play with them.

Actually, he didn't play with the small robots; studied them. When they were all out of his backpack, he counted them. *Eleven jellborgs*, he thought. *On my last trip to the Middle East, I gave up one robot. This time, I gained eleven. Not bad.*

Of course, Yaakov reminded himself that the jellborgs didn't belong to him; Bobby the Brute had pilfered them from the ocean, and someday they would have to be returned to their rightful owners. No matter; although Yaakov didn't like the idea of using the robots for any purpose before he could return them, he thought that maybe they could come in handy in some way.

As he tinkered with the jellborgs, he quickly discovered that their motion wasn't limited to water; they were also able to use their tentacles to walk on flat surfaces. In addition, even though they didn't seem to respond to voice commands (at least not from Yaakov's voice, and spoken in English), Yaakov was able to train them to march in a line.

Since Yaakov knew that these little inventions mimicked real jellyfish, and had already managed to hunt down imitation blood in the Red Sea, he decided to test their reaction to real blood. He peeled off his old bandage, washed his wound, and applied a new bandage with more of his antibiotic ointment. Then, he threw the old bandage across the tent and appointed one jellyfish to be the Line Leader. He held Line Leader on the tent floor, "facing" the old, bloodstained bandage, and let go of it with both hands.

To Yaakov's fascination, Line Leader marched across the tent, found the bandage and began to suck up the blood that had been absorbed in it. The other ten jellyfish followed Line Leader, and instantly joined the feast. Within two minutes, the used bandage was quite dry. After their meal, the artificial jellyfish simply marched around the tent, appearing confused.

Next, Yaakov decided to test the robots' electric shock capabilities. This function, as Dilip Sitoop had explained, was the jellborg's ability to simulate the stings delivered by real jellyfish. The shocks were not designed to cause lasting damage to any person or animal; they were simply meant to give a hint: "Back off." Fear could be effective at stopping or slowing down an enemy, as Yaakov had learned on the *Pacific Dreamer*. Rahulla Allijabulla had been seen in Timna Park, and Yaakov wanted to be ready to confront him, if necessary. *What else do real living things give off, possibly attracting animals such as real jellyfish?* he wondered, looking around the tent. Eventually, his eyes alighted on a small container of deodorant that stuck out of his father's duffle bag. He now had his answer: sweat.

There was certainly no short supply of sweat in Timna Park that day. Yaakov checked his watch for the current time and temperature. At 4:00 in the afternoon, the temperature had fallen to only 105 degrees Fahrenheit. Perhaps, by 4:00 AM, it would be down below 100. Yaakov pulled off his right sock, turned it inside out, and tossed it across the tent. Then, once again, he placed Line Leader at the head of the jellborg parade and turned it loose. Amazingly, the robot propelled itself straight across the tent floor, found the sweaty sock, and began to sting it with mild electrical impulses. As Line Leader moved, the other jellborgs followed it closely behind. They, too, soon began to shock that sock. With each impulse, the sock moved several inches away from the little robot that had shocked it, only to be attacked by another one nearby. Before long, the crowd of jellborgs looked like a bunch of kids playing beach volleyball. It was certainly the most entertaining show that Yaakov had seen in a while.

Yaakov observed the robots' antics until he had lost track of time. Before he knew it, his show was interrupted by his father's jolly voice.

"We're back!" Yehuda greeted his son, lifting the canvas tent's flap and poking his head inside.

Yosef followed closely behind Yehuda. He leapt into the tent, and flopped onto the sleeping bag next to Yaakov's. Then, he lay back, rested his head on a pillow, and let out a sigh of exhaustion. "No sign of that little thing, and I'm tired of looking for it."

Yehuda came inside and sat down on the remaining sleeping bag. He grabbed two bottles of water from the pack next to him, and handed one to Yosef. Neither he nor Yosef seemed to notice the little robotic performance in the corner.

Yaakov soon heard the voices of his mother and sister, as they returned to the adjacent tent.

"Yeah," said Yehuda, facing Yaakov directly, "we looked everywhere, and I mean *everywhere*. We retraced every step that you could have taken, in every spot that you told us about, and that thing was nowhere to be found. We even hiked all the way over to Slaves' Hill. That's what they call the King Solomon's Mines area. There were a bunch of security guards over there – you know, because of the big dig tomorrow – and none of them took us seriously when we told them what we were looking for. So, we're fresh out of ideas."

"And," added Yosef from his makeshift bed, "we also checked out the Mushroom. I don't mean the one that you and me saw, where Rahulla was. I mean the one that's just called 'The Mushroom.' We couldn't find anything there. No bombs, nothing."

"So, maybe the whole thing is a hoax," said Yaakov, trying to comfort himself with the possibility that no bombs had been set in the first place.

"Maybe," said Yehuda.

"Well, we'd better leave this place soon," remarked Yosef, "in case it isn't. If there are any bombs, I don't want to be here tomorrow when they go off. And besides, what if we're still here when they do, and then the security people come looking for us, because we knew so much about them ahead of time? Maybe they'll think we were behind the whole thing."

"And while they're coming after us," replied Yaakov, "Rahulla Allijabulla gets to jump into the Mines and grab whatever he can find, so he can make off with his fortune. I think you're right, Yosef. We can't stay here forever."

Yosef suddenly sat up straight. "Hey, what's that noise?" he asked.

"Look," replied Yaakov, feeling a bit smug and pointing to the gathering of robotic jellyfish in the corner. They couldn't seem to get enough of Yaakov's sock. "I got those things to sting my sock."

Yosef shook his head in obvious disbelief. "Wow, you had way too much time on your hands this afternoon."

"Actually," said Yaakov, in a matter-of-fact tone, "you'd be surprised what those things can do."

"Like what?" asked Yosef.

"Well," answered Yaakov, "while you were away, I figured out how to control them. They've got little switches and buttons. You can only really see them up close. I got the robots to march in a long line, and to attack a specific target. They even sucked up the blood from my old bandage."

"Oh, that's gross," said Yosef, making a disgusted face. He lay back down and turned his back toward Yaakov. "I'm taking a nap."

Just then, Rachel and Leah poked their heads into the tent. While Yosef faced the wall and rested, Yaakov spoke to his mother and sister in a near-whisper, explaining what he had succeeded in getting the robotic jellyfish to do. He also demonstrated those feats, leading a parade of jellborgs outside and getting them to sting a little green shrub that stood in their way. Rachel cracked up in laughter, while Leah simply stared with an open mouth.

The rest of the afternoon was rather uneventful. Leah set up her easel and paints in order to capture the surrounding desert scene in a painting while there was still time. As the sun continued its descent in the Negev Desert sky, and shadows everywhere grew longer, Yaakov stood by his mother's side and watched her produce a magnificent landscape. He was amazed by what she could produce in such a brief span of time. Later, the Peretzes lounged in their tents and discussed their plans for a while, all agreeing that it would be dangerous to remain at Timna Park much longer. If Bobby the Brute had told the truth, then his time bombs were set to explode at some time in the morning. They needed to get up early and escape the chaos before it happened.

Yosef awoke from his nap just in time for dinner. Grilled hot dogs and other treats were followed by afternoon and evening prayers, then by bedtime stories. Finally, everyone lay down to sleep, including Yosef.

There was no sleep for Yaakov, though. He simply

reclined on his mat, listening to the howl of warm desert winds and the steady rhythms of his father's and brother's breathing beside him, while Leah and Rachel slumbered in the adjacent tent.

Nighttime provided little relief from the scorching desert temperatures. With the constant thirst, there was little chance for Yaakov even to snooze anyway, but it was especially hard for him to fall asleep with such a load on his mind. He kept asking himself how he could have been so foolish as to take that little fob out of his backpack and drop it somewhere, without noticing where it had gone. Yaakov repeatedly retraced his steps and actions in his mind, feeling guiltier each time that he re-imagined the paths that he had walked that day and the things that he had done. He struggled to remember everything, and asked himself over and over again where the small device could have fallen. So much seemed to depend on it!

Yaakov lay there in the dark and stared at the tent ceiling until he could no longer bear the discomfort and the feeling that he had failed. He didn't even want to sleep; to fall asleep would be to give up. How could he simply hand Rahulla Allijabulla a victory, by letting him cause destruction and steal a piece of history?

Finally, he sat up, found his shoes, put them on, and slipped quietly outside, grabbing his backpack on the way out. *I have to stop Rahulla*, he thought.

In a cloudless sky, the moon cast a brilliant light across Timna Valley Park, making it quite easy for Yaakov to see the desert around him. Just a few days had passed since the middle of the Jewish month, so the moon was still nearly full. He turned on his flashlight anyway, pointing it towards the ground near his feet and trying not to disturb the other campers. At the moment, only a slight tinge of pain reminded Yaakov what had happened to his left leg on the previous day. For an instant, he imagined his parents' scolding, along with his siblings' complaints of "No fair! Why does Yaakov get away with everything?" Then, he was off.

The path closest to the campsite was a cycling trail. As his map showed, the trail headed in a generally northwest direction, passing the Temple of Hathor before joining the paved road. A quick stroll down this road, with no cyclers or siblings to distract him, and his flashlight to guide the way, was all that he would need. Only Yaakov was truly able to re-imagine everything that had happened near the old Egyptian ruin. If he stood near it and quietly tried to remember every detail of what had happened there that day, then it should be a cinch to locate the missing fob. The fact that he was breaking the park rules by strolling on this path after closing time was just a detail.

Before long, the Temple of Hathor came into view. He shined his flashlight toward the structure, and then suddenly noticed a faint whirring noise in the distance. The noise seemed to be getting louder by the second. Was somebody looking for him? Quickly, he turned off the flashlight and began to look around frantically for a place to hide. If only he could reach Solomon's Pillars, the massive boulders that towered next to the ruined Egyptian temple!

Forgetting about his leg injury, Yaakov left the trail and began running toward the Pillars. The noise continued to grow louder, though. What was that noise, anyway? he wondered. It was too faint to be a motor vehicle, and there weren't many plants in the area to be trimmed by a gardener's leaf-cutter. He stopped running and turned around to take another look at the trail. Right away, he spotted the source of the mysterious whirring noise. It was a robot, moving slowly down the bike path under its own power.

Yaakov began jogging back toward the trail, to take a closer look at the moving robot. For the moment, he forgot about the lost fob. By the time he reached the trail, the robot had passed him, but it was easy for him to catch up to it by running at a mild pace. Soon, he was keeping up with the robot, running alongside it as it made its way down the cycling trail. This robot was a bit shorter than Yaakov, and was built with a small set of wheels that allowed it to ride along the ground. Apart from the wheels, it was a fairly humanoid machine. Its basically spherical head included a roundish face and two lights that shone down onto the ground in front of it.

Entertained by his new discovery, Yaakov decided to study it. To understand it better, he had to stop it in its tracks. He quickened his running pace for a few seconds, passed the robot, and then jumped in front of it. When it approached him, he held out his hands and grabbed it, preventing it from moving any further while its wheels spun uselessly underneath it. Almost immediately, he heard a human-like voice coming from the robot's insides. It said something in rapid-fire Hebrew, using some unfamiliar words. Then, it spoke in English, apparently repeating its message.

"The park is now closed to visitors," said the robot. "Please return to your campsite or find the exit immediately." This message was then repeated in Arabic.

A patrolling park robot! thought Yaakov. *This thing might come in handy.*

Since the robot was on patrol, Yaakov reasoned that it must have a way to communicate with the park's security staff, in order to alert them to suspicious people, objects or events. To get any help from his new robot friend, Yaakov needed a way to communicate with it. If only there were a way to use his BotConv, that handy device that had served him so well earlier that summer...

Still grasping the patrol robot by its face, Yaakov held his flashlight in his left hand and shined it across the top of its head. He searched for a small number that was likely imprinted somewhere on the machine's body, in a somewhat obvious spot. All BotConv devices were connected to the International Robot Communications Network, or IRCN. The IRCN attached a code to every robot that could be commanded using a BotConv device. This robot's IRCN code was what Yaakov needed.

He squinted while scouring the patrol robot's head and body for its IRCN code. He felt rushed as he did so, because the park security department would certainly take notice if one of their robots arrived late back at its base, wherever that was. Also, he really wasn't supposed to have stolen away from his family that night; in the back of his mind, he knew that what he was doing was unsafe and rather foolish. His right arm was getting tired, too.

After about two minutes, the robot let out another recorded warning, in the same three languages as the previous one. "The park is now closed to visitors," it said. "Please find your way back to your campsite or exit the park immediately. Security will be notified of all trespassers. You will receive a citation."

Great, thought Yaakov. *That's all I need right now: a citation.*

Finally, he spotted some tiny raised black markings imprinted alongside a couple of plug-in ports on the black surface of the robot's back. An electrical outlet rested next to another socket resembling a primitive USB port that he had seen in old pictures. Using his flashlight, Yaakov carefully read the letters "IRCN" next to a sequence of several numbers and English capital letters. He repeated the code to himself, under his breath, until he had memorized it. Then he let go of the robot, which continued on its way. Still standing on the bike path, Yaakov pulled his BotConv out of his backpack. He entered the IRCN code into his BotConv and stored it in the little gadget's memory. Next, he attached the BotConv to his left ear.

Now, it was time to attract the patrol robot and the park security staff to the Mushroom and a Half. If the security staff's own robot told them that there was something amiss there, then perhaps they would actually search that area for Bobby the Brute's hidden time bombs. An idea began to form in Yaakov's mind.

He took another look at his map, located the Mushroom and a Half, and proceeded to walk in that general direction, using his flashlight to light the way. He felt afraid of his surroundings and of what he might find at the Mushroom and a Half, but forced himself to continue walking anyway. As he walked, he dared not look at his watch. *I need to do this*, he kept telling himself, as we went.

After what seemed like nearly an hour, he passed the

familiar landmark known as Spiral Hill, and finally spotted a pair of sandstone structures that he recognized: the Mushroom and a Half. Both stone formations cast long shadows in the moonlight. He stopped for a moment to catch his breath, sipped some water from a bottle, and took another look at the path ahead of him. Yaakov had approached this site using the same route that he taken earlier that day with his brother. It was a path that skirted the Half. By walking along this path, the two brothers had been able to hide behind that stone while observing Rahulla Allijabulla's actions at the Mushroom.

Tonight, the day's scene seemed close to repeating itself. A lone figure wearing a flimsy-looking sunhat stood between the Mushroom and the Half, with his back toward Yaakov. He was facing the Mushroom and waving a little flashlight in front of him, apparently searching for something.

Yaakov froze in his place as soon as he saw the man. Then, he quietly took a single step in the man's direction. The man instantly spun around, faced Yaakov, and shone his flashlight directly at him. There was no mistaking the man's identity: Rahulla Allijabulla.

"What are you doing out so late, boy?" he barked. His voice matched those of Captain Saway and Raul, the mysterious stranger who had called Yehuda's cell phone earlier in the week to harass the Peretz family.

"What are *you* doing out so late?" retorted Yaakov defiantly. He felt no fear.

"I've got work to do. And you know something? I've been a little impatient with Bobby lately. I don't want to wait 'til tomorrow morning for his explosions. I'm gonna set them to go off tonight! Thanks for leaving that little gift for me by the Temple of Hathor." With those biting words, Rahulla pulled a small object from his pants pocket and waved it in front of Yaakov, taunting him. It was the missing fob.

Without thinking, Yaakov rushed straight toward Rahulla and jumped into the air, attempting to grab the fob from the criminal's hand. Just a second too soon, Rahulla pulled it away from Yaakov and held it over his own head. Yaakov landed on the ground in front of Rahulla. As he hit the dirt, he felt a new surge of pain radiating up his injured left leg. His backpack was still unzipped, with its main opening facing Rahulla. Some water bottles and other items instantly flew out of it and scattered in various directions. One of those items was Yaakov's plastic bag full of fake blood. The bag smashed into a rock, breaking open and spewing its reddish contents all over Rahulla and the surrounding sand.

"Awww," said Rahulla, in a slow, mocking tone. "Did someone spill his little backpack? It's too bad you have no digging robots to help you tonight."

The Peretz family's digging robot had foiled Rahulla's most recent plot, in Djerba, by trapping Bobby the Brute.

"You're right," replied Yaakov, in a calm and cocksure tone, despite his intense pain. "No digging robots tonight, *Captain Saway*. Instead, I brought something even better."

"What?" asked Rahulla, his voice dripping with contempt.

"Jellyfish."

Yaakov effortlessly pulled Line Leader out of his

backpack, aimed it at Rahulla, and set it in motion. The robotic jellyfish led the way, and was instantly joined by all of the others. Rahulla's mouth dropped open as the assault began. A swarm of jellborgs quickly jumped onto Rahulla and began to climb all over him, stinging him with repeated electric shocks as they licked up the delicious substance that had stained his clothing and skin. Howling in anguish, Rahulla soon dropped Bobby the Brute's fob.

Quickly, Yaakov pulled himself up and limped over to the dropped fob, still carrying his backpack in one hand. He picked up the fob, closed his backpack, and then tossed it somewhere behind the Mushroom. He didn't know where it landed, and didn't care. Then, he tapped the BotConv attached to his left ear.

"*Chefetz chashud*," he said, "*etzel ha'Pitriyah va'Chetzi*." Those Hebrew words meant "Suspicious package, next to the Mushroom and a Half."

As Rahulla continued to groan and whimper in pain, Yaakov made his way to the Mushroom. There, he immediately found the detonator, took a brief look at the fob's current passcode, and began to enter it on the detonator's small touch-screen. As soon as he had entered the seventh number, a brilliant flash of white light lit up the night. At the same instant, an unfamiliar loud voice screamed a sudden order at him in Israeli-accented English.

"Freeze! Both of you!" came the shout, from behind Yaakov. "Turned around and face me! Now!"

Yaakov dropped the fob, raised both hands and turned around slowly. He saw three park security guards in a little jeep with its headlights on. All three guards held their handguns and aimed them in

Yaakov's direction.

"You two, come with us," said one of the guards.

The next thing he knew, Yaakov found himself sitting next to Rahulla Allijabulla, being driven away from the Mushroom and a Half.

Busted for trespassing, Yaakov thought. *Some vacation.*

10 THE MISSING PIECE

The imposing park ranger named Oror banged his fist into the wooden desk in front of him and yelled something that sounded threatening in speedy Hebrew at Rahulla Allijabulla, who sat next to Yaakov on a black folding chair. Two fellow rangers, Amir and Shai, stood by, carefully monitoring their captives. Rahulla simply stared blankly ahead, enduring the rant without reacting to it in any visible manner. Yaakov understood some words of Oror's words, but the ranger definitely spoke too quickly to enable Yaakov to catch everything.

When the ranger was finished, Rahulla looked up at him and calmly repeated the now-familiar, dull phrase that everyone in the ranger station had already heard about a dozen times that night: "*Ani lo mayveen.*" ("I don't understand.")

Yaakov had heard of this phenomenon before. His parents had sometimes explained to him that, in practically every country in the world, some individuals who commit crimes will try to escape punishment by claiming that they don't understand that country's language or the questions that they have been asked. In fact, the park rangers only knew Rahulla's name because Yaakov had identified him on their arrival at the ranger station. Yaakov himself knew enough Hebrew to understand some of the rangers' questions and dialogue. He decided that it was smarter and safer to cooperate than to pretend he didn't know what was happening around him. Besides, the park rangers spoke English fairly well.

Oror sat down behind his desk, leaned towards Rahulla, and switched to thickly accented English. "Maybe you understand your little friend's language. I will talk slow. What were you doing tonight at the Mushroom and a Half?"

Predictably, Rahulla gave his usual response. "*Ani lo mayveen,*" he said, in an emotionless tone.

"Maybe he knows Arabic," suggested Shai, in Hebrew.

"Why not?" replied Oror, with a shrug.

Shai snapped his fingers in front of Rahulla's face. To Yaakov's surprise, Rahulla turned his head toward Shai and looked directly at him. Shai asked him a question in Arabic.

"*Ani lo mayveen,*" answered Rahulla.

The three rangers exchanged some words amongst each other for about a minute, while Yaakov sat quietly and wondered how long it would take for his scheme to work. Then, they went back to interrogating Rahulla.

"You don't understand Hebrew," said Oror, staring at Rahulla with a menacing look, "you don't understand English, and you don't understand Arabic. What do you understand?"

"*Ani lo mayveen*," repeated Rahulla.

Oror let out an exasperated sigh and rolled his eyes at the ceiling. Then, he addressed Yaakov. "And tell me again what you were doing there," he said.

Yaakov spoke slowly and tried to sound as clear as possible. "I was trying to stop Rahulla Allijabulla from setting off a time bomb. That device stuck in the Mushroom is a detonator with a timer. Its controls were locked with a temporary code that kept changing. Rahulla had the controller with the code on it, and was trying to use it to reset the time bomb to go off later tonight. I managed to get the controller from him, and unlocked the detonator with the code. Then, I wanted to turn off the detonator, so that no bombs would explode at all."

"How did you know there were any bombs set to explode?" asked Shai.

All three rangers listened intently as Yaakov patiently explained everything that he knew about Rahulla Allijabulla, Bobby the Brute and their plot. He told them about the threat to Tzadok Sapir, the voyage to Anacapa Island, his kidnaping, his escape, and the discovery of the plot to set off bombs in Timna Valley Park and to rob King Solomon's Mines of any ancient treasures that may still lie buried underground. He showed the park rangers his leg wound, adding the full story of how he and his brother had found Bobby the Brute's little fob controller and stolen robotic jellyfish, and how they had replaced the real controller with their phony one. Finally, he explained everything that he remembered about the past day's experience in Timna Park, including his family's failed searches for the real fob and his recent encounter with Rahulla. Throughout the story, Rahulla simply sat and stared blankly at the floor.

Amir tapped Rahulla on the shoulder. Rahulla moved his head slightly in Amir's direction.

"*Mah atah omer*?" ("What do you say?") asked Amir.

Rahulla simply parroted his usual stock answer: "*Ani lo mayveen.*"

Amir briefly looked at the other two rangers. "*Meshugayim*," he told them. Yaakov certainly recognized that Hebrew word, and understood its meaning: "Crazy people."

He then turned his attention to Yaakov. "It's a crazy story. Why we should believe you? Maybe this guy's your uncle, and you two just went outside to bothering something." Amir's "bothering" sounded like "*buzzer-ring.*"

Yaakov began to sweat. He needed a way to clear his own name, to pin all the blame on Rahulla, and to stop those explosives from going off. *Think fast*, he told himself, *and speak slowly. Think fast and speak slowly.* He sat back, took a deep breath and began.

"This man is definitely not my uncle," he said, trying to sound as calm as possible. "He's not even my relative. I don't know him. But I know something about him. Like I just told you, he is a thief. He wants to set off an explosion in the park, later tonight, using the bombs that another thief already planted somewhere in the park."

The three park rangers looked at Yaakov for a moment that felt like a month. Finally, Oror spoke.

"Maybe we can believe you, " he said, "if you just

show us where they are. You say there are bombs? Where?"

Where, indeed, were Bobby the Brute's bombs? That question had been bothering Yaakov since he had first learned of that scoundrel's cruel scheme, and he still had no answer. It was the missing piece of this entire mystery, the final element that would solve the riddle.

Just then, a quick buzzing noise came from the left pocket of Oror's pants. He pulled out a mobile device, checked its screen for a second, and then looked at the other two rangers.

"*Chefetz chashud*," he told them. That expression, meaning "suspicious package," was the same one that Yaakov had told the patrol robot a short while earlier.

"*Ayfo?*" ("Where?") asked Shai.

"*Ha-pitriya va-Chetzi*," ("The Mushroom and a Half") he replied.

"We have robots that go and check the park at night," said Oror, facing Yaakov, who pretended to be learning this information for the first time. "That's how we found you. There were people around after closing time. Just now, one robot found a strange package at the Mushroom and a Half. Is that what you mean?"

An idea instantly sprang into Yaakov's mind. He scolded himself momentarily for not having thought of it before. Had he been alone, he would have smacked himself on the forehead.

Yaakov sat up straight in his chair and answered the park ranger confidently. "I don't think that's Bobby the Brute's bomb, but it's the right place to look for it."

"We have to go there now and check it out anyway," said Shai. "And we have to call the bomb squad. So where are these bombs you keeping telling us about?"

Yaakov calmly and directly addressed Shai. "In the Half."

Before long, Yaakov found himself sitting once again in that loud, rickety little jeep with Amir and Oror, while Shai remained at the ranger station and kept close watch on Rahulla Allijabulla. As he rode, Yaakov thought about the big picture. The missing piece of the puzzle had just fallen into place. Those bombs had to be buried somehow, somewhere, inside the Half.

It all made perfect sense now. Back on Anacapa Island, Bobby the Brute had spoken very truthfully to Rahulla Allijabulla, the only person capable of helping him. Bobby's complaints about the food at prison were honest ones, the very first remarks that had come to mind. So, he spat those words out of his mouth just as quickly as the awful mushroom soup that he had been forced to eat for dinner every miserable night while imprisoned in Tunisia. Having already decided to complain about the mushroom soup, Bobby also decided to hurl a jab at the prison cook, calling him "a jerk and a half." Revenge against the mushrooms alone wouldn't have tasted sweet enough; Bobby had to get back at that cook, too, whom he despised even more than the soup. To get back at both the mushroom soup and its hated cook, Bobby hid the detonator in the Mushroom and the explosives in the Half. The gross, inedible dish would symbolically destroy its maker.

The jeep approached the Mushroom and a Half, and Yaakov soon saw what a mess he had created with his "suspicious package" ploy. A sizable area around the pair of giant sandstone formations had been roped off with yellow police "caution" tape. Official-looking vehicles were parked nearby, and electric lights glared at the stones and their surroundings. At least half a dozen bomb squad officers were busy examining Yaakov's backpack from afar, some of them poking it with ten-foot poles and others controlling small robots that actually touched and probed the backpack closely.

Amir parked the vehicle at a safe distance and turned off its headlights. He and his passengers stepped out of the jeep. Oror tapped Yaakov's arm and pointed at the backpack.

"This is the bomb?" he asked Yaakov. "It's inside that pack?"

Yaakov shook his head vigorously. "No, there's nothing dangerous in there. I…left my backpack when I came here a little while ago. If you want those guys to find the bombs that I told you about, they need to check the Half."

Oror gave Yaakov a now-familiar look. It was the look that meant, "You're wasting my time with silly stories." Then, he walked over to the taped-off area and began to chat with the nearest officer. After about a minute, another officer picked up a megaphone and spoke into it.

"*Zeh rak yalkut. Ayn bo shoom davar*," he announced. Yaakov understood those words: "This is only a backpack. There's nothing in it."

The officer who had just spoken to Oror then led several others to the Half, along with their bomb-seeking robots and other specialized equipment. They immediately got to work. Yaakov followed them from afar. He stood in one spot, about twenty feet from the police "Caution" tape, and watched all of the activity, waiting on pins and needles for his prediction to come true.

After several tense minutes, the bomb squad began making their announcements. Yaakov and the park rangers listened closely. Buried deeply within three of the deep holes that marked the outer surface of the Half, the bomb squad had discovered C4 charges wired to infrared sensors. C4, as Oror explained to Yaakov, is the name of a plastic explosive, a soft, moldable material used mainly by engineers to demolish obstacles. On some occasions, terrorists have also used this material to cause enormous damage and to inflict suffering.

Oror extended a large hand to Yaakov, and Yaakov shook it.

"Good work, *chabibi* ("my friend")," said Oror. "Now, we have to leave the bomb guys to do their job." He called his fellow ranger. "Amir, *bo, naylech*!" ("Amir, come, let's go!")

Just then, Yaakov's phone rang. He sheepishly pulled it out of his pocket, recognized his mother's number on its screen, and braced himself for the coming chew-out session and lecture.

"Hello?" he answered.

"Where are you?" screamed Leah, so loudly that Yaakov had to pull the phone a few inches away from his ear to protect his eardrum.

"I'm at the Mushroom and a Half."

"What?" hollered Leah. "Are you crazy? What are you doing there? It's the middle of the night! You know how dangerous it is to sneak out alone like that! What in the world were you thinking?"

Yaakov took a deep breath. "Imma," he answered, slowly, "it's okay. I'm here with the park rangers and the bomb squad. They just…"

"*The bomb squad*?" she interrupted, hysterically. "What *in the world* is going on?"

"Imma, please just hear me out. They caught Rahulla Allijabulla, and they found the bombs. They were hidden inside the Half. Really deeply. There's no way we would have found them by ourselves. Wait, hold on for a minute."

He looked over at Amir and Oror. "Can you guys give me a ride back to the campsite?"

"Why not?" Amir replied, with a shrug.

"Thanks." The three of them walked back to the jeep. As they got in, Yaakov put the phone back to his ear. "Imma, the rangers are giving me a ride back to the campsite," he said. "There's a lot to tell now. Here goes."

As they rode back to the campsite, Yaakov related all that had happened to him that night. His mother interjected comments along the way, like "That was foolish," "Why did you have to go out by yourself?" and "Never confront an adult alone like that!" Nevertheless, he managed to get through the entire tale over the course of the ride.

The rangers dropped him off with a hearty "Shalom" ("Peace" and a common greeting), wishes that he enjoy the rest of his stay at Timna Park, and assurances that he needn't worry about anything. His mother greeted him with more verbal missiles, which he barely heard, due to his exhaustion. Yaakov stumbled into the guys' tent, collapsed onto his mat, and drifted into the deepest slumber that he had slept in a long time.

He was the last member of the family to wake up the next morning. Slowly, he pulled himself from his sleeping bag and made his way outside. *It must still be early,* he thought. *It only feels like eighty degrees.* Leah and Rachel's tent was already packed. Yehuda and Leah were seated on a park bench, busily discussing their plans for the coming days.

"Good morning, son!" greeted Yehuda, in his usual jovial manner. "I heard about your little adventure last night. Exciting!"

"Hello, Abba," replied Yaakov, meekly. "Yeah, it was…strange."

Yehuda got up from the bench, walked over to Yaakov, and placed an arm around his shoulder.

"Don't worry about anything," he told his son, quickly. "Imma told me the whole story. It's a new day. We're past it now. Just be a little more careful next time."

Yaakov looked up at his father. "Okay, Abba."

"Imma, what are we doing today?" called Yosef from a distant desert shrub, where he and Rachel had apparently invented some kind of weird game.

"Abba and I have a couple of surprises in store for you kids," she answered. "First, we're going to go and watch the big dig. It's open for people to see what the archaeologists uncover at King Solomon's Mines."

"And what else?" asked Rachel, loudly, while running excitedly toward her mother.

Leah smiled. "We'll tell you in a little while. But first, let's finish up breakfast and hurry over to Slaves' Hill, where they're about to start digging."

Yaakov hurriedly washed up, rushed through his usual morning prayers, and hurriedly consumed a cupful of instant oatmeal. Then, the family made their way to Slaves' Hill.

They found the area packed with researchers,

tourists, local politicians, and reporters. Everyone gathered around the excavation pit, where a team of about a dozen archaeologists carefully dug through the dirt and examined every item that they found. The Peretzes huddled together, as close to the actual excavation pit as possible. After about fifteen minutes, a murmur began circulating through the crowd. The chief archaeologist soon emerged from the pit and stood on a makeshift podium. She picked up her smartphone, launched a microphone app, and began to speak into it.

"We are finding some extraordinary things here." Yaakov recognized her voice. She was none other than Dr. Orit Levi-Iparon, the speaker on the audio tour that Yaakov and his family had heard on their way into the park the day before. "First of all," Dr. Levi-Iparon announced, "there's a lot of slag, which is rock left over after the ancients extracted copper from the copper ore surrounding it. Also, we are finding more bones from fish and other animals, like camels and goats. There are many more animal bones here than we ever expected. It looks like they ate a lot of goat meat while they sat here and worked. Apparently, some of the so-called 'slaves' who worked here at Slaves' Hill were actually fed very well. Not only that, but they ate off of nice utensils. For the first time, we are discovering things like brass bowls and forks. We even uncovered a plate with engraved letters that spelled, *'l'Yaakov'* 'belonging to Yaakov.' That must have been the name of a worker who did a lot of copper smelting."

"I'm proud of you, Yaakov," Leah told her son, while the professor continued her announcement. "Listen to all of the things that you've saved from those awful thieves. It's all part of our history, real treasures from the past."

"Imma, can we go now?" asked Yosef. "It's hot out here, and I'm getting bored just standing around."

"Sure," answered Leah. They turned and began walking back toward their campsite.

"How did this big guy get so good at catching pirates and gangsters?" asked Yehuda, soon after they had started down a trail.

"Perhaps," answered Leah, "he's still got a bit of that piracy in his blood. They say it takes one to know one. Well, maybe it also takes one to catch one. Did you know that I'm an eighteenth generation descendant of a pirate?"

"Really?" wondered Yosef aloud.

"Which one?" exclaimed Yaakov, excitedly.

"His name was Samuel Pallache," answered Leah, "and I heard many stories about him growing up. He lived over 400 years ago. Piracy was legal at that time, just about everywhere. So Samuel went out and raided Spanish ships. A lot of people say that he was trying to get back at Spain for the Inquisition. Anyway, I can tell you more stories about him later." She stopped walking for a moment, paused, and turned to her husband, who had also stopped. "What do you think, Yehuda? Should I tell them about what we had in mind for today?"

"Sure," said Yehuda.

Leah resumed walking and speaking, while the children followed her. "Kids, we talked to Aharon Sapir this morning. Of course, he was really excited to hear about all that happened lately. He also invited us to stay at his villa in Tiberias for a few days. He even texted us a picture. It's a beautiful place, overlooking Lake Kineret. That's an enormous lake that looks more like a sea. All the maps call it the 'Sea of Galilee.' It's all the way in the north of the country, and we'd have to leave soon to get there by tonight."

"Oh, Imma, I don't want to travel all the way there," Yosef grumbled. "Can't we just stay around here for a while?"

"You'll like it in Tiberias!" she answered. "There's a lot to do there."

"Do we really have to go there, Imma?" Yosef whined.

"I'll tell you what," said Leah, in a calm and reassuring voice. "We'll stay here for a little while, and maybe take an easy hike around. Then, it's off to the north. I'm telling you, you will really enjoy the Kineret." She stopped for a second and looked at Yaakov. "Now that we've gotten our pirate adventure out of the way, it's time for a real vacation."

ABOUT THE AUTHOR

Nathaniel Wyckoff was born and raised in the beautiful San Fernando Valley of Southern California. From an early age, he was profoundly interested in reading, writing, telling, and listening to stories.

Though he works in a technical field, he counts storytelling among his favorite activities. Nathaniel's storytelling career took flight with the births of his children. His children enjoy all kinds of stories, but most of Nathaniel's stories for them involve zany adventures and confrontations with wacky bullies. Nathaniel's first novel, *Yaakov the Pirate Hunter*, was inspired by his son's request for a story about robots. It combines elements of science, adventure, and Nathaniel's beloved Jewish tradition. As the Peretz Family Adventures Series continues, Nathaniel's children continue to serve as a source of inspiration.

In addition to writing, the author also enjoys studying his Jewish traditions, reading, playing the accordion and the piano for his family, playing games and sports with his children, and taking his family on hiking trips, camping trips and other adventures.

Join my email list, for updates on future books:
http://www.peretzadventures.com

Made in the USA
Monee, IL
28 April 2022

95571097R00085